To Glenys, Grey, Jody, and Herb—
time stood still
in the backseat
on the way
to Red Mountain

CONTENTS

BLACK CROWS

You have to wait for good things to happen—wait and wait and work so hard—but bad things occur out of the blue, like fire alarms triggered in the dead of night, blaring randomly, a shock of sound, a chatter of current from which there is no turning back.

There's only the day that starts like any other, and when it ends, it leaves you shaken, wobbly, unsure of where you stand, the patch of ground that holds your feet dissolving, disintegrating from under you. Often there's a sign, a harbinger of what's to come. Sometimes there are many signs, like black crows scattered in the road, but they blend into the scenery on the path ahead. You can only spot them when you look back.

CHAPTER 1
A CLOCK STOPS

My mom says worry is like a leaky faucet—every drip makes you imagine something bad on the way . . . trouble . . . trouble . . . trouble . . . do something . . . do something . . . do something.

But when you're twelve and the only guy in the house, you're responsible for an awful lot. It isn't just catching mice and taking out the garbage either. You've got to be aware.

My sisters don't worry at all. And my mother? She keeps her concerns to herself. When I ask her what's wrong she just says nothing . . . nothing . . . nothing.

Still, the evidence is stacking up. The phone rings and my mom dives for it when the caller ID says *Home*

Fi, short for Home Finance, which is the people we pay for our house. At dinner there's mac and cheese and spaghetti and soup—but never chicken, steak, or take-out Chinese. And when it's team night, there's no money for pizza. I have to borrow from my six-year-old sister, Mouse, who counts five bucks from the dimes she tapes to the inside of her shoe.

My older sister, India, has her head in girl world. On a good day, she resembles the crabby cafeteria lady who guards the ketchup with the voice of God. On a bad day . . . let's not go there.

It's amazing how little penetrates India's head. She doesn't see how jumpy Mom is. She doesn't notice how Mom spends all her time on her cell under the McFad-dens' big oak tree. Sure, the reception in our house is iffy, but we have a landline . . . why wouldn't she use that?

Mom's not limping or coughing or skipping meals. There are no new doctor appointments on the calendar. But nothing else is written down either.

India rolls her eyes when she talks to me about this. "She put the calendar online, Finn, get a grip, you're like a little old man the way you worry."

"She hasn't been using her credit cards either, have you noticed that?"

"We're broke." India shrugs. "What's new about that?"

There's no telling what Mouse makes of all this. Mouse is like Einstein on a sugar high. If Emily Dickin-son and Galileo had a kid, that would be Mouse.

And then there's Bing, her invisible friend. We've told her scientists don't have invisible friends, but she insists we're wrong. I don't know where she gets her information. Do all invisible friends know each other? Is there a clearinghouse for invisible facts? A social network? A chat room? These are the kind of questions you find yourself asking around Mouse.

On the other hand, it makes sense that Mouse's best friend is imaginary. What other six-year-old thinks the Internet is the secret way zeroes travel at night and the problem with prime numbers is they can't have babies.

And together, how do Mouse and India get along . . . like two sheets of sandpaper rubbing against each other.

Still, part of me keeps hoping India is right. Maybe we are just broke . . . which isn't that unusual.

I'm headed for the kitchen to pour myself a bowl of cereal—it's a little-known fact that guys can't think without cereal. Only, all that's left is one lone piece of shredded wheat so stale you could build a bunker with it. I toss the box in the recycling and Mouse pounces on me. She's holding a picture she made of the backyard with our dog, Henry, and my basketball hoop. All of the refrigerator space down low is taken, so she orders me to put her drawing under the top magnet where my mom keeps PTA forms and permission slips.

That's when I see how many field trip forms are late. My mom is a teacher. She gets everything back on time.

I track her down walking back from the McFaddens', cell in hand.

"Mom." I wave the permission slips in her face.

She nods as if she understands.

My mom has long, straight brown hair like India's and the same brown eyes as her too—big like in cartoons—only people don't stare at her the way they stare at India. Coach P. said that's because India's "drop-dead gorgeous."

Not what I want to hear. It would be a lot easier to keep an ugly sister out of trouble, believe me.

Mouse takes after our father's side of the family. Her hair is a mess of red curls like a football helmet two sizes too large for her tiny freckled face. I resemble both sides: straight brownish reddish hair, lighter skin than my mom's and India's, but not freckly like Mouse. I'm short too—we're all short.

I could grow, though. It could happen. If you're a short basketball player, you have to be three times better than anybody else. I'm not three times better than everyone else—not even close . . . but I'm working on it.

I'm out there every morning before school doing drills, and I go to practice every afternoon. I help out so I don't have to pay the league fees. I *make myself useful,* as my mom always suggests. I keep track of the water and the snacks and the drills we do each day. If Coach P. needs help rolling the basketball hoops to the parking lot to create an extra court, I'm the guy.

At school I'm the person you borrow an eraser from or call for the homework assignment. Don't get me wrong. I'm not a teacher's pet or anything. Kids like me okay. If you're inviting a bunch of kids, you include me, but if you're inviting one, I'm never the one. Everybody knows my first name: Finn. No one knows my last name: Tompkins.

We're inside now and my mom's scanning the kitchen, her eyes skittering from cupboard to cupboard as if she's developed a nervous tic. Oh no! What if she has MS? She's not going to up and die on us like Dad did. Is she?

"What's the matter?" I ask her.

She holds her breath, then lets the air out in a nervous burst. "Family meeting."

Family meeting? Why couldn't she just have said *nothing*, like she usually does?

I try not to hyperventilate as we head for the living room, which is also the den, the dining room, and my mom's bedroom.

Mouse is skipping and hopping next to Mom. In Mouse World, family meetings are fun.

"India." My mom raps on the bathroom door.

"Do you mind? I'm peeing," India snarls.

"No she's not," Mouse calls. "She flushed already."

"Shut up, Mouse!" India shouts, tossing something against the door—the toilet paper roll probably, but a minute later the knob turns and she's out. The skin around her nose is red and irritated as if it's been freshly tortured.

Mouse is jumping around like Tigger, and India is

picking at her zits. At least my sisters are acting normal.

Mouse snuggles next to Mom on the sofa bed. I sit in the overstuffed chair with Henry curled at my feet. Henry is part German shepherd, part who knows what else. The shelter said she was a boy, which is why we named her Henry. You would think the shelter would know the difference.

India doesn't sit anywhere. She wants to be able to make a quick exit. Quick exits are her specialty. "I have homework," she announces. "How long is this going to last?"

"I didn't tell," Mouse whispers to Mom.

"Good girl." Mom squeezes her hand, but her voice sounds as if it has been pounded flat.

"Didn't tell what?" I ask.

"About the moving boxes," Mouse says.

Moving boxes!

My mom's eyes dart to me. She takes a ragged breath. "I should have told you sooner. I kept hoping I could make it go away."

India scowls. "Make *what* go away?"

"We're moving to Colorado. Fort Baker, just outside of Denver. We're going to live with your uncle Red."

"WHAT?" The question explodes out of India's mouth.

My mother clears her throat. "We're losing the house."

"What do you mean *losing*?" India demands.

"The bank is taking it."

The words enter my brain, making me feel distant, as

if my ears need to pop. My mom couldn't have said we are losing our house, could she?

"Banks don't own houses," Mouse says. "Otherwise our mailbox would say BANK OF AMERICA and it doesn't, it says TOMPKINS. That's how the mailman knows where we live. Five-four-one Morales Street, Thousand Oaks, California."

"Shut up!" India hisses.

"India," Mom warns, her fingers automatically forming bunny ears, which is her school's hand sign for quiet. "Mouse is just trying to understand in her own way. Now hear me out, all of you.

"This house isn't ours anymore. We can't live here." She waits, letting her words sink in. "You can't believe how hard I tried to work out a deal with the bank. I kept us here through the holidays. We had Christmas in our own house, but—"

"We always have Christmas in our own house," Mouse interrupts. "Where else would we have Christmas?"

"But why are we going to Colorado?" I manage to speak through the wind tunnel in my head.

My mother's left eyelid begins to twitch. "Uncle Red has a lot of room and he really wants us to come."

"Uncle Red? I hardly remember Uncle Red," India says.

"You liked him. Both of you did." Mom nods to India and me.

"I liked him when I was six. What difference does

that make? I'm not moving to some stupid hick state," India snaps.

Mouse raises her hand, waves it in front of my mom. "Did I like him? What about me?"

"Just let me finish, all right?"

Mouse climbs up on Mom's lap. "Bing doesn't remember Uncle Red. He's worried Uncle Red won't be nice. But I told him Mommy's going to be there. Mommy is nice."

Mom runs her tongue over the edge of her teeth. "I will be there . . . but not right away."

The room is suddenly quiet. Not even the clock is ticking. We all stare at her.

"Where will you be?" I ask.

"I'm going to stay with Aunt Sammy and Uncle Tito. I have to finish the school year. If I leave them high and dry mid-semester, I'll never get another teaching job—not only that, I'm not accredited to teach in Fort Baker. In the summer I can take the classes I need to get credentialed in Colorado."

"You're shipping us off by ourselves to some uncle we hardly know?" India asks.

"Look, I'm not going to lie to you. This is going to be hard on everybody. But Uncle Red is happy to have us coming. He's been calling every day full of ideas for how we'll get settled in with him. He's putting up a basketball hoop." She tries to smile at me. "He's found a poster of the planets for Mouse and a place where the teenagers all go."

"A poster and a hamburger stand . . . that's supposed to make us feel better?" India asks.

"India, do you think I did this on purpose?"

India's eyes register the break in my mom's voice. "No," she mutters.

My throat is so tight I can hardly swallow. "When exactly are we leaving?"

My mom takes a deep breath. "You're flying out tomorrow night. Uncle Red has arranged to have you picked up at the Denver airport."

Now we all talk at once—pelt her with reasons why this is impossible. The game next week, battle of the books, outdoor ed, the oath I signed for Coach P.'s team. Some party India's going to with Maddy. Bing doesn't have time to pack. We need to stop the clock so he won't have to hurry.

Mom lets us wind down.

"Tomorrow night," India squeaks. "That's a joke, right?"

Mom shakes her head slowly as if she doesn't want to jiggle her brains.

"Look, this makes no sense." India's voice is suddenly reasonable. "We can't leave in the middle of the school year, any more than you can. We'll all stay with Aunt Sammy and Uncle Tito."

My mom shakes her head, harder this time. "No room."

Aunt Sammy's house is tiny; one room on top of another, each one smaller than the last. All the boys sleep in one room, Aunt Sammy and Uncle Tito in the other. But if I can't stay in my own home, I'd rather be at Aunt Sammy's house than any other place in the world.

"I can sleep in the boys' room on the beanbag chair. I do it all the time," I tell her.

"I'm staying with Finn on the beanbag chair," Mouse announces.

"Thanks a lot," India snaps.

"Finn's nicer than you are," Mouse tells her.

"Stop! This is hard enough without you two fighting. Finn, you can't stay at Aunt Sammy's. You will all three stay together, no matter what."

"You heard them. They don't want me. I'll stay with Maddy," India insists. But she must know Mom will never agree to this. She won't even allow double sleepovers.

"Mouse needs you," Mom says.

"Mouse can't stand me."

"She's right. I can't stand her," Mouse agrees.

Henry's cowering under the coffee table. She hates it when we fight. I run my hand down her fur to the spot under her chin she likes me to scratch. "It's okay, Henry," I say as she puts her big paw over my hand to keep it there. That's when my heart stops cold. "Henry! What about Henry?"

"She needs a ticket," Mouse offers.

"You need a special traveling crate and shots, Mom. Remember when you had that kid in your class that moved to Hawaii? He had to put his dog in quarantine for three months. Remember?"

10

"I remember," she mutters.

"We can't just take Henry to the airport tomorrow night."

"No, we can't," she agrees quickly—too quickly.

"Mom, have you even checked into this?" I ask.

"We'll wait until Henry can go too," Mouse suggests. "Then Bing will have time to pack."

Mom's chin sinks down below her shoulders. "It might be better if we found Henry a new home." She croaks the words out.

We stare at her as if she's just suggested we run over our grandma.

"Henry is a part of our family," I say.

"Even homeless people have dogs," India declares.

"India Jena Tompkins, don't make this worse than it already is." My mom's voice rises.

"She's our dog, Mom," I whisper.

"Okay, okay . . . I'll try and find a way to bring her," Mom concedes, "but not tomorrow night."

I can't eat, can't sleep after that. The truth is so much worse than anything I imagined. No home, no dog, no basketball, no Coach P., no more California. Not even my mother. This can't be happening. It just can't.

INDIA

CHAPTER 2
THE BROKEN LOCK

What a joke last night was. That stupid family meeting—I mean, my mother land-mines our whole life, then she's like *Okay, who wants egg rolls?* I wish I had it on video. I'd post it and get a million hits. What would I call it? *Psycho Mom and the Moo-shu Pork, episode one.*

She's going to change her mind. Of course she is. We're not leaving tomorrow—oh, excuse me, *today* . . . that just can't be.

I can hear Finn moving something heavy out in the hall. This is so crazy . . . we can't move all our stuff in twenty-four hours. I get under the covers and pull the pillow over my head. All last night Mom was like:

"Colorado is so beautiful. The mountains are incredible!!! You'll love the outdoorsy lifestyle!!!"

She has brochures from the travel agency. We're being kicked out of our house and she's playing tour guide? I wish she'd get a grip.

But when I call her on it, she gives me the same stupid old line: *When life gives you lemons, make lemonade.*

What if I don't like lemonade? What if I'd rather drink cyanide?

There's always a cute saying from Mom. Something teachery and ohmygod so corny.

The woman doesn't get it. All she cares about are grades, saving money, and a clean stovetop. When Finn was little he gave her a sponge for Christmas. And she loved it! Is that sad, or what?

Finn totally kisses up to Mom, which makes me want to puke. Mouse would too if she weren't so clueless. Mouse is like a mutant child from the Nature Channel. Where did she come from?

Thank God for Maddy. She totally gets what it's like to live here. She calls Mom "Rules," Mouse "the Demon Child," and Finn "Mr. Personality" because he's so quiet.

Mom left me alone last night, but this morning she's been all over me. She tried sending Mouse in to drag me out of bed. That didn't work, so now she's coming after me herself. "India." She raps her knuckles on my door.

I bury my head under the pillow.

"India, this is happening whether we like it or not."

I take the pillow off. "Mom, call the bank. That guy. Remember, you said *that guy* would help."

A few weeks ago I heard her and Aunt Sammy talking about the problems she was having with the house. She said she was getting help from some company person guy. I figured she had it covered, but apparently not.

Mom opens the door, walks in, and sits down on my bed, looking at Mouse's side of the room, which is a disaster area. She probably lost her stupid planet book again.

It isn't possible that this room will no longer be ours.

My mom is talking again. I try to concentrate on what she's saying. "And then he took our money and ran."

"Call the police then, Mom. Don't *move*."

"Call the police." She shakes her head.

"You paid money to some guy's company to restructure the loan, right? He's the one who should be taking care of this."

"Look, I shouldn't have trusted him. I got scared and . . . that made everything worse, but this probably would have happened anyway. I need to explain it all, every last thing clear down to the fine print—especially the fine print, but I can't now, honey. Now we've got to move."

"Why'd you wait until the last minute to tell us? You'd kill me if I did that."

"The last minute . . ." She sighs. "This has been going on for six months. We've had four hundred last minutes. Every time, I patched it back together again.

14

I didn't want you and Finn and Mouse to live with this hanging over your heads. Can you imagine how Finn would worry? He'd have been a wreck."

"Oh yes, poor Finn." I get so tired of hearing about Finn and how he worries, and Mouse and how hard it is for her to be a child genius.

"It's not just Finn, it's you too, honey. I didn't want any of you to worry, but there's nothing to be done about it now. Yesterday morning we lost the house. It's final. This is the end of one chapter and the beginning of another."

"We're never going to live here again?"

"We're never going to live here again."

"But what about Ariana's party? We'll be back for that, right?"

"India, honey, don't you understand what I'm saying?"

"Sure I understand." I snort. "Why do you always think I'm stupid? One C in French and all of a sudden I'm an idiot."

"I don't think you're stupid. I just think sometimes you believe in your own wishful thinking."

"Mom, I totally get it. You've ruined my life."

She pulls at the small hairs that are sticking out of her ponytail. "I know this is hard, India."

"Why do we have to live in Fort Baker? We could get an apartment here. Did you ever think of that?"

"At Uncle Red's we won't have to pay rent. It will give me a chance to push the reset button."

"I'll help out more. I'll get a job. You made this decision without even talking to us."

15

"If I'd known six months ago what I know now, I would have done things differently. But I didn't know and I wasn't about to drag you kids into it . . ."

"I'm not a kid, Mom!"

"I know you're not." She massages her temple with her thumb. "And I'm asking you to take on grown-up responsibilities. Can you handle that?"

"You never think I can handle anything."

"Oh, India." She sighs a long, sputtering sigh. "Look, will you just get dressed and help Mouse get packed?"

When she's finally gone, I find my cell and head straight for the bathroom. I lock the door, but the stupid lock falls off in my hand.

I flip open my cell. There are fifteen texts from Maddy. As soon as I turn my phone on, she calls me, which means she's seriously mad.

"In, I've texted you a billion times. What's wrong? It's that rotten reception at your house, right?"

"Uh-huh," I mutter.

"Why didn't you go down the street to the McFaddens' tree? The one you said was like magic."

"I never said it was magic."

"Whatever. Look, you're mad, aren't you? Has the Demon Child been making up stories about me again?"

"No."

"It's the party then, right? Ariana said you could come. I told you that. It's only because she thinks Brendan is a hottie and he likes you that she didn't invite you in the first place."

16

"Maddy, I'm not mad. I just had stuff to do for my mom." I try to make this sound light, like it's no big deal.

The line goes quiet. So quiet I figure the call got dropped and I'm going to have to go out on the street, when Maddy says: "You are such a bad liar, In."

"I'm not lying."

She snorts. "For weeks we've been talking about Ariana's party and how you didn't get invited and now I get you invited and you treat me like dog waste."

"Maddy, I didn't treat you like dog waste, I'm sorry I didn't text. It's just . . . there's something going on," I whisper.

"Well, what is it?"

"I can't talk about it right now."

"I thought we were best friends. I mean, should I be calling Lizzie? Because she would so tell me everything."

"India." My mom bangs on the bathroom door. "Let's get going!"

"Maddy, look, my mom's gone nuts. I gotta go."

"Oh great . . . she's not going to call up my mother again, is she?"

"No. Nothing like that."

Maddy sighs. "I don't know what I'd do if I had your mom, and don't even let me get started on the Demon Child. But we're good, right? You'd tell me if we're not."

"Totally."

I want to tell Maddy what's happening, I really do,

but she'd drop me for Lizzie in a hot second. Lizzie hangs around waiting for that too—hoping I get mono or something. Maddy is a good friend, she really is. She just can't stand to be alone.

This isn't permanent, anyway. I'm not going to live out in the middle of nowhere.

Never going to happen. Never.

FINN

CHAPTER 3
OUR EX-HOUSE

Everything is a jumble, all mixed up and upside down. We're looking for suitcases, cramming stuff into bags to be sent later, boxes to be mailed, bins to go to storage, garbage bags to be thrown out. There is no time for anything and no way to begin to get everything packed.

How's she going to move the rest of our stuff by herself?

"Mom, you can't do this alone. Why don't we fly tomorrow?"

"I already bought the tickets," she tells me as I wedge one more plastic crate into our jam-packed little car and somehow manage to get the passenger's-side door closed.

"I'll be fine," she mutters as she gets in the car and backs out of our parking place.

Not even the parking place will be ours anymore, I think as I watch her leave.

I was right all along . . . something bad *was* happening. Being right stinks.

While my mom makes a run to the storage locker, we stay home trying to decide what to put in the one suitcase we are each allowed to bring. Any more and they'll charge us extra, and my mother wants her last fifty dollars to give to India so we'll have money for the trip. I have seven dollars to my name, which I put in my suitcase. Mouse has the dimes in her shoe.

The only real estate we own now is what we can fit inside our roller bags.

"How does she look to you?" I ask India.

"God, Finn, she's fine," India says. "Our life is falling apart and you're worried about Mom?"

"Yeah, I am . . . can you imagine?"

She rolls her eyes.

Mouse is helping to pack stuff with a running commentary about the stuff itself and not the fact we're moving it—*Here's the book about the black holes. The Bermuda Triangle is not a black hole. It's not, Finn! Did you know that?*

She doesn't seem to get the fact that we're moving. She hasn't said a word to Bing about the flight. Usually she discusses everything with him. That's how you know what's going on with her.

The only thing that gives any inkling she knows what's happening is she wants to dig up her goldfish graves and take the skeletons along.

"Do you have to be weird all the time?" India snaps at Mouse.

I glare at her.

"I'm sorry. It's just not normal to want to haul around the skeletons of your pets," India says.

"It's not just my pets; if they were your bones, I'd want to dig them up too," Mouse says as she locates a trowel under a stack of naked Barbies.

"Oh, well, I'm flattered then," India answers, her voice thick with sarcasm.

Mouse marches out to our tiny yard, which is the size of four sidewalk squares and has three plants and a basketball hoop.

"Are you just going to let her do that?" India asks me.

"Mouse," I suggest, "let's leave the fish bones for last, okay?"

"Okay." Mouse nods agreeably.

India glares at her. She wants Mouse to like her better than me, but India is mean to Mouse. She blames Mouse for everything. What does India expect?

I can't worry about that right now. I have problems of my own . . . I've got to call Coach P. and let him know what's going on. I can't just disappear on him. What kind of a person does that?

I have his cell number, and it's not like everybody does. Just Logan, MC, and me! Of course, they're tall, but never mind that.

I'm hoping to leave a message, but on the third ring Coach P. picks up. "Finn, my man, what's up?"

It feels good to hear his voice. I forgot about that part.

"Uh, oh, hi, Coach. Look, I just wanted to . . ."

"Wanted to what? Spit it out, Finn."

I push through the lump in my throat. "To say goodbye. I'm moving to, uh, Colorado today."

"Finn . . . *today*? Why?"

I can't tell him our house got repoed. That makes me sound like the biggest loser in the world. "My mom wants to," I mumble.

"Oh, your mom . . ." he says as if this explains everything. Coach P. thinks women are irrational. "Well, look guy, will we get to see you before you go?"

"I dunno," I mutter.

"Okay then . . . we'll miss you. Nobody can eat those hot dogs like you can."

"Coach . . . I don't, ummm, eat a lot. You're thinking of Logan."

"Logan, yeah, how many did he eat on Spirit Day?"

"Nine."

"Nine . . . amazing. Well, Finn. You're a good guy and a good sport. Keep in touch and come back and visit me, okay?"

"Coach?"

"Yeah, son."

"You think I'll ever be a good player?"

He sucks in a big breath. "Sure, sure, why not? Like I always say: Keep your head in the game and your eye on the ball. Now, you take care of yourself, Finn. Don't do anything I wouldn't do." He laughs his big laugh.

The line is dead now, but his words circle around inside my head.

Sure, sure, why not . . . sure, sure, why not.

That's not the same as yes, is it?

I get my basketball out of my suitcase and dunk it from the place where I always make it. Not from the spot where I don't.

"You okay, Finn?" my mom asks when she gets back.

I pretend I don't hear her.

"Let's call Uncle Red. He really is excited about you coming. The girls too . . ." Her voice trails off.

I still don't answer. Just keep dunking the ball from my sure-bet spot.

When we're finally ready and Mouse is sent to do a last pit stop, India corners Mom.

"Mouse should stay with you," she says.

My mother winces. "I know," she admits, "but I don't like her around your cousins and their music."

"You're sending us off to live with a strange relative because you're worried about a few bad words?" India asks. "It's not like she hasn't heard them before."

"India, I'm doing the best I can here," my mom tells her.

"I just don't think this decision makes sense," India reasons.

"Mouse drives Uncle Tito up a tree with all her questions," my mom whispers.

"Uncle Tito is an adult and he can't deal with her. How are we supposed to?"

"She's your sister, India," Mom says as she slams the hatchback closed a final time.

Mouse appears at the back door. She looks at India and my mother. "It's me again, Bing . . . isn't it?"

The hardest thing is saying good-bye to Henry. Henry is like the Christmas tree at Christmas. The birthday cake on your birthday and trick-or-treating on Halloween . . . we love her that much.

After she takes us to the airport, my mother will come back and pick Henry up along with our last loads of stuff. I know she will . . . but Henry doesn't. Henry goes into stealth mode. She slinks out the door and makes a mad dash for the car.

We try and get her back in the house the usual way, filling our pockets with Milk-Bones, but she lies on her back with her paws up and refuses to move. My mother gets the leftover Chinese—her last splurge— and dribbles the beef with broccoli in a path from the car to the house, but Henry doesn't fall for it.

The only thing that works is when all four of us lock the car door and walk back into the house as if we're coming home again. Then when Henry follows us, my mom quick shuts her inside. The last thing I see as we drive away is Henry's big brown eyes watching through the front window of our ex-house.

CHAPTER 4
AIRPORT EXPLOSION

Ever since I found out they kicked Pluto out of the planets, I have not been feeling so sure about a lot of things.

If they can decide Pluto is not a planet all of a sudden like that, things are not being run the right way up top. Pluto is a planet in *My Solar System* on page one, page six, and all of chapter three.

My brother, Finn, who has no pimples, says that's because Pluto is a dwarf star, but Finn is wrong about this. Finn is wrong about a lot of things, but I keep quiet about how many. He is a nice big brother and I don't want to ruin him.

My sister, India, is fourteen and she's only nice when

Mommy makes her. India says when she gets her driver's permit, she will attach a leash to my belt loop and make me run behind the car.

India and Mommy are way ahead of Finn and me. Neither of them is paying any attention because they are talking a lot. They probably haven't read the airport signs. Mommy says I am the official sign reader in the family. I want to go back and make sure I understand the one about liquids. 3:1:1: three liquids, one ounce, one bag, but Finn is pulling me along by my blue corduroy belt loop. He says I took too long reading the monitor about the flights coming and the flights going, and now we're late.

India is ahead of Mommy. India likes to be first. She's a big hog about it too. They are up front in the line near the conveyor belt.

"Shoes off, put them in the bin," Mommy says. She's not flying today on account of she likes her sixth graders better than us.

"Finn," I whisper. "We have a problem here."

"Mom!" Finn calls to our mom, who is walking through the metal detector. "Mouse has to go to the bathroom."

"All right, you people, I've got a flight to catch," a man with green socks growls. His black roller bag bumps my blue bag in not a nice way.

"Can you wait?" Mommy asks from the land on the other side of the metal detector.

"I DON'T HAVE TO GO!" I shout so she will hear.

Mom's cheeks turn pink. "Come on then." She mouths the words and waves me on.

"Take your shoes off," Finn says.

I pull on his arm and he bends his knees so I can whisper in his ear. "Someone might steal my money."

Finn whisks the hair out of his eyes faster than usual, which means I am making him nervous. "Just take your shoes off. No one cares about your dimes."

I don't like to make Finn nervous. Maybe it wasn't such a good idea to take all the underpants and socks out of my suitcase and put in my special mints and soda explosion ingredients and my baking soda and vinegar volcano. But Mom said I have to make a good expression for Uncle Red. A volcano makes a good expression, that's for sure.

My blue plaid roller bag is going through the X-ray machine. The man with the green socks takes cuts. Hey . . . grown-ups are not supposed to take cuts . . . are they?

"Come on through." A man in a uniform with an important yellow badge wiggles his bright blue-gloved fingers at me and I walk through the pretend door frame of the metal detector, which is also made of metal. This does not make sense. How come it doesn't make its own self go off?

There's an orange light over the X-ray machine like the lights on the police cars, and the lady looking at the X-ray pictures is smacking her gum.

I tried to get Mommy to let Bing take his own bag, but she said Bing doesn't have a ticket. She should have gotten Bing his own ticket. He likes it better when he has his own seat.

"Marvin, open up the blue one," the X-ray lady says.

I am on the land on the other side of the metal detector now. Mommy unties my blue sneakers so I can put them on again. Her fingers hold the dimes taped inside.

India is nowhere. Probably Mom let her go ahead to buy gum. India always gets to do the fun things.

"Do I need to show Bing's wallet?" I ask.

Bing uses my dad's old wallet. He has important stuff in there like identification and one real dollar.

My mom shakes her head.

Mommy had to show hers to get a special pass on account of she doesn't have a ticket and she isn't going anywhere. Marvin has my roller bag. I duck under the cord to have a little talk with him.

"Marvin," I say. "There's a little explosion stuff in there, which I need to show Uncle Red. He doesn't have kids, you know."

Marvin's droopy red eyelids stop drooping.

"Mouse." Mommy grabs my shirt. "You're not supposed to be over there."

"Call for backup. We've got a nine-one-one on the blue suitcase," Marvin tells the X-ray lady. He points his finger in my face. "You come with me."

I'm trying hard to subtract the time of our plane from

the time on my mouse watch, but I don't know how to carry over in my head. "Marvin," I tell him, "our plane is leaving in forty-five or twenty minutes."

But Marvin isn't listening. More and more people with yellow badges are around us. I try to see if all the badges are the same or if it's like when India was in Girl Scouts and they were all different.

My mommy holds tight to my hand. "She stays with me," Mommy says.

Marvin shakes his head.

Mommy presses Finn's fingers around my arm and motions to Marvin. She and Marvin move away so I can't hear, but Mommy is talking in her big important teacher way. People do what Mommy wants.

Marvin shakes his head. Mommy tells him something else. Marvin shakes his head harder.

"Finn," Mommy says, "let Mouse go. Mouse, this man is going to ask you some questions, that's all."

"Come with me," Marvin commands.

I don't want to go with Marvin, but Mommy is nodding like I need to help her on this. She wants me to straighten the problem out. This is what I explain to Bing.

Sometimes I talk to Bing out loud and sometimes I talk to him in my head. Bing doesn't need sound to hear.

Bing and I follow Marvin to a small room in the back. Marvin takes a stack of magazines off the orange bucket chair and picks up his clipboard.

I do not like being way back here with Bing and

Marvin. What is Marvin going to ask? I try to think of every answer I know.

"Name?" Marvin says.

"Geneva Tompkins, but everybody calls me Mouse on account of I'm good at squeaking. Want to hear?"

Marvin shakes his head. "You're traveling with your mother."

"No," I say. "We've used up all our money. Mommy has to work because that's how she gets more. Is that how you get more, Marvin?"

Marvin writes this down on his clipboard. "Who exactly are you traveling with?"

"My sister, India, and my brother, Finn. India, Geneva, and Finland. Two countries and a city. That's me." I raise my hand. "My mother wanted to travel, but instead she had kids."

This is my one grown-up joke. I got it from India. Marvin doesn't laugh.

"And your father?" Marvin asks.

"He died when I was in Mommy's tummy. I couldn't see him on account of there was skin in the way. But Bing saw him. He took a picture for me."

"Who is Bing?"

"He's my friend."

"Did you pack your own suitcase?"

"My mom and India did, only I made a few corrections."

"Which means?"

31

"I added the explosives," I whisper.

His face looks suddenly the color of my snot when Mommy says I have to stay home from school. "Explosives?"

"Have you ever seen mints explode? You put them in soda and *PFFFFFFFFFF*." I make my best explosion noise, but it's not as good as Finn's.

"This is some kind of science experiment?" His voice squeaks.

"Oh, no. I don't have science yet. Not until third grade."

Marvin shakes his head and makes grunting noises. "Do you understand you aren't allowed to bring liquids on the plane? Liquids like vinegar, liquids like soda."

"I would have understood if Finn let me read the whole sign, but he said we had to—"

"You stay here," he snaps before I even finish explaining.

When Marvin comes back, Mommy, Finn, and India are with him. Marvin hands me my suitcase. It's very light. He's taken all the good stuff out.

My mom hugs me like I have been away a long time.

"How am I supposed to control her? That's why Maddy calls her the Demon Child. Plus she lies," India tells Mommy as we all hurry up.

"No she doesn't," Mommy says.

"She lied about Maddy."

"Ancient history, India, come on. I thought we agreed

not to talk about that anymore. Now, let's go. We gotta hustle here."

We are in the land on the other side of the metal detector again. My mom is half running, pulling me along to gate number thirty-seven, where she bustles us into the "C" line.

"What if she took out her underwear like she did when we went to Grandma's?" India yells. "What'll she wear?"

"You'll have to let her borrow some of yours," Mommy answers.

"No," I say, "India's are too small." The bigger you get, the smaller your undies. I do not understand this.

"She can't borrow mine. Let her wear Finn's," India snaps.

"INDIA! *Boy's* underwear!" India is sickening sometimes. I feel like biting her. I did that once when I was really mad, but my mom took away my peanut butter and honey sandwiches for one whole week.

"Uncle Red's then?"

"IN-DIA!" I stop in my tracks in front of the magazine stand.

"Did you take them out?" India demands. "Because if you did, you'll have to borrow Uncle Red's!"

I punch her then. There's nothing else to do.

Mommy gets in the middle so India can't punch me back. Usually Finn does this, but he doesn't like underwear talk. He's pretending he isn't our brother right now.

"That is the last of that! The next time I see you two,

you will be treating each other with respect, you understand me?" Mommy tells both of us.

The "C" line is moving up to the ticket lady. Mommy squats down so she can look into my eyes. She smells like oranges and crackers. "Mouse, you understand what's happened?"

"I wasn't supposed to bring the science explosion stuff."

"That's right." She nods. "And where are you going?"

"Uncle Red's house."

I know everything. I never miss even one on my tests at school. India says that's because kindergarten is so easy. No one misses any problems in kindergarten, but Mommy has been giving me tests for fifth graders and I never miss any on those either. India doesn't like to hear about that.

"Look, sweetie, you're going to have to be a really good girl at Uncle Red's. You'll need to mind India and Finn and Uncle Red. Can you do that? I will call you every night and I will come as soon as I can."

My shoulders slump low down. I feel low down too. "How long is *as soon as I can*?"

"Three months."

"How many hours is that?"

My mom brushes my hair back with her hand. "A lot of hours. Too many to count."

"I could count. I'm a very good counter. Do you want me to? I know! How about if I stand right here and wait for you? I could sit down when I got tired."

We are up at the very front of the "C" line now. India hands all three of our tickets to the airline lady in the blue skirt.

"You'll have fun at Uncle Red's. You will," Mommy says.

Bing is nodding his head. He thinks it's going to be fun too. I hate when he sides with Mommy.

Mommy hugs Finn and India, but she leaves the last hug for me. My face is smushed up in Mommy's shirt, so my voice is smushy too. "Are you sure you can't come now?"

Mommy nods the for-sure way. Not the maybe way.

I pucker my lip and do my sad puppy face. "Will you at least wave from the window?" I ask.

"I promise, sweetheart. I will wave from the window." Mommy's lips get shaky. Bing says she's trying not to cry.

MOUSE

CHAPTER 5
MY SOLAR SYSTEM

Inside the plane there is a row of little windows. I try every window. I have to find the one that has Mommy in it.

"Did you need something, young lady?" a big pinky person asks as I slide between her knees.

"Mouse!" India grabs my blue corduroy pocket. These are my favorite of all my blue corduroys. She better not rip them, you know.

"I'm sorry, ma'am." Finn jumps between me and India. His face is all red like Elmo's. "Mouse, get out of there!"

"At least say excuse me," India hisses in my ear.

A flight attendant lady in a blue skirt wants to look at our boarding passes. "This is first class," she says. "You

36

are in coach." She points to the back of the plane.

"Coaches are from the olden days," I tell her. "We are in an airplane."

The flight attendant's little wrinkles all come together. She doesn't understand. Sometimes I have to think up another way to say the things in my head. But the flight attendant moves on. She doesn't want to hear another way. I talk to India instead.

"I can't see Mommy from any of the windows. That plane is blocking us. India, you have to ask the plane to move. Make sure you say please *the nice way*," I whisper. Sometimes when India says please, it sounds like a naughty word.

"Don't be crazy," India snaps.

"I promised to wave. Bing promised to wave." He never breaks his promises, not ever, and I usually don't either, only sometimes.

"Mouse, I can't get the plane to move."

"Let's try from that window." Finn points to a window where there are no passengers in the seats.

But that window doesn't have Mommy in it either.

"Mouse, c'mon. She's not there!" India yanks my pocket so hard it rips a little.

"I can't sit down without waving to Mommy. She will wait forever trying to wave. She could die without my wave."

"We'll call her when we get to Denver." India drags me back.

I don't want to sit down. Bing doesn't want to sit down, but India has on her mean look. Way, way in the backety back she finds our seats. "You sit there, Mouse, in case you have to pee," India commands, pointing at the aisle. "Finn, you're there." She points at the middle. That means she gets the window. Didn't I tell you she hogs everything?

Finn grunts. I don't think he likes the middle, but he's supposed to keep us from fighting. Mommy said.

India throws her stuff on the seat but doesn't sit down. She takes out her cell and walks to the front of the plane so we won't hear her talking to Maddy. I sure hope Maddy isn't coming with us.

Finn lifts all of our suitcases up and wiggles them into the overhead compartments on account of Mommy says he's the man of the house.

I sit down on my seat and I read the sign. *Fasten seat belt while seated,* it says. How else could you do it, I wonder.

When I'm all buckled in and my markers and paper are ready in front of me, I look at the man in the seat across the aisle. He has an almost bald head except for a few baby hairs in the middle. I think I know him. I look down at his feet and I see his green socks. This is the man who butted in front of me.

"Oh, it's you," I tell him, when he sees me staring at him. "You're the one who took cuts."

"Excuse me?" he asks.

"In line. You took cuts. I saw you."

He rolls his eyes. "Lotta kids on this flight," he mumbles, raising his book up like he cannot wait to read the next page.

38

I pop up in my seat to count how many. "Six kids and one baby is not a lot. A lot is twenty."

He ignores me.

"It's okay about the cuts," I whisper. "I don't care. It's Bing who keeps track."

I think he's not going to answer. His book is hiding his face, but then the cover comes down a little. He points to my brother, who is sunken down in his seat. "That's Bing?"

"No. That's Finn."

"Who's Bing?"

"He's my friend," I say.

"Oh," the man says, looking all around. "Where is he?"

"Right here." I point to Bing.

The man nods. He has a tiny smile on his face.

"You don't believe me, do you?" I ask. "Do you want to see his ID?"

The man shakes his head. "That won't be necessary," he says. "Bing is an old-fashioned name. How'd he get the name Bing?"

"I dunno. I didn't name him. His mother named him."

"His invisible mother?"

"I never met his mother. I don't know if she's invisible or not."

"Well, I'm sorry, Bing," the man with the green socks says, though he isn't looking at Bing at all. "Will that do?" he asks me.

"Yes," I say. "That was very nice. Where are you going?"

"Denver."

"Denver! Hey Finn." I jiggle Finn's arm. "The man with the green socks is going to Denver too."

"That's where the plane is flying, Mouse."

"Oh. Yeah." I turn back to the man with the green socks. "Of course you're flying to Denver," I tell him.

The man with the green socks laughs.

I look at my mouse watch. "Do you know what time it is there?"

"It's one hour forward."

I shake my head. "Time isn't supposed to move around like that."

"I don't like it either," he agrees. "I do a lot of flying and I never get used to it. The sky will be blue as can be, but your watch says it's midnight. Midnight where you used to be. Eight in the morning where you're going. Who can keep track?"

I understand about not getting used to things. Pluto is one of those things I'm not used to either. Nobody has been able to tell me one good reason why he's not a planet. Not one. Then I think an awful thought. What if *My Solar System* isn't in my suitcase? What if Marvin has it right now and he's blacking Pluto out of the book?

"Finn, Finn! Could you get my suitcase down? What if Marvin has my book?"

"Who is Marvin?" Finn asks. The man with the green socks looks at me like he wants to know too.

40

"Finn, c'mon . . . pleeeeeease. All you have to do is pull up that metal thingy, see right there, right up there, and then the bin pops open—"

Finn's head doesn't move, only his eyes look sideways at me. "India will kill us," he whispers.

I don't care about stupid old India. It's Pluto that's important. "C'mon Finnnnnn," I plead.

He makes a grumbling noise in his throat, but he unsnaps his seat belt, stands up, opens the bin, and pulls down my suitcase.

"I get to unzipper it. *I do*. Let me!" I shout.

Finn puts his hands up like he surrenders. I unsnap my seat belt and unzipper the bag. Inside is my toothbrush, my other blue corduroys, my shirt, and my favorite pajamas. No socks. No underwear. No explosion equipment and no *My Solar System*.

All I can think about is Marvin and his permanent marker blacking Pluto out of the book. "I have to get *My Solar System*," I let Finn know. Mommy says you're always supposed to *let people know* where you're going.

Finn's eyes get big. "Mouse, no!" he shouts, but I'm already running down the aisle, between the plane seats—running hard like I'm on the playground racing Jimmy T. I'm beating him too when suddenly, *bang*. India is smack in front of me. Her eyes have gone wild.

"GO . . . SIT . . . BACK . . . DOWN!" The fringe on India's vest shakes with each word. She points back down the aisle.

41

"But India, I have to—"

"Sit down and do not get up again or I will *call the police*." She flips open her cell phone, her green fingernails hover over the buttons.

"You can't call the police on your *own sister*," I tell her.

"Try me."

"You won't get your learner's permit if we get in trouble with the police," I say.

Her head goes sideways. Her eyes get squinty and mean. "You *really* want to be the one to keep me from getting my learner's permit?"

"No." I shake my head as big as it will shake. India follows me to my seat stepping on the back of my shoe, she's walking so close.

Finn doesn't say one word now. Is it because he is worried about Uncle Red? Or is it because pimples are poisoning his brain? Every morning I check Finn for pimples and he doesn't have any, but India says there are invisible pimples that grow under your skin. I'm not sure what I'll do if pimple pus turns Finn mean, like what happened with India.

Now I have to go to the bathroom. But I don't want to go in a strange bathroom, so I hold it like at school. I will hold it until we get back from Uncle Red's. I only like the toilet paper at home.

FINN

CHAPTER 6
TIME CHANGE

Will Mom be okay for so long by herself? Will she go to my cousins' basketball games? Will she eat with Aunt Sammy and Uncle Tito? What if she can't get a job in Colorado? What if she decides to stay in California?

Will there be a basketball team in Fort Baker? Is it too late to get on it? Should I have asked Coach P. for a recommendation? Does Uncle Red like basketball? What kind of a hoop did he get?

"India?" I ask. But India ignores me. She's busy texting Maddy. Sometimes it seems like Maddy is a computer virus that has taken over India's brain. Although

Maddy can be nice too. Last year this kid named Connor was picking on all the sixth graders, and Maddy clobbered him. She's the only eighth-grade girl who would do that.

Mouse isn't worried about Uncle Red's. She's worried about the plane flight. She is standing in the aisle asking the flight attendant questions. How many wheels does the plane have? What happens if there's a flat tire? If you fly through a cloud and all you see is white, how does the pilot know which way to steer?

The flight attendant tells Mouse to buckle in, we are about to take off.

"If it weren't for you I'd be at Aunt Sammy's right now," India growls at Mouse.

"Where would you sleep?" Mouse asks.

"In the living room."

"Under the foosball table? Or by the lamp cord? If you're by the lamp cord, the door will hit your head when someone comes in. And then Aunt Sammy and Uncle Tito and all our cousins will see your birthmark. I see it when you're asleep. I always look."

"Sleeping is private. Do not look at me while I'm sleeping!" India is practically shouting. "And keep your nose away from my birthmark."

"It's not that bad, India. Bing thinks it looks like a kangaroo."

"Like I care about Bing's opinion. Uncle Red isn't going to want you any more than Uncle Tito did. Who wants a kid who's going to blow up the living room?"

44

"I'm not going to blow up the living room!"

"Shhh! We're not supposed to talk about that kind of stuff on an airplane. We'll be arrested," I tell them.

"She's the one who started it." Mouse points at India. "And anyway, I wanted to show him because he has probably never seen a pretend volcano."

India rolls her eyes. "Oh yeah, like that's a priority for him."

"Look, we're about to take off," I say, hoping to distract them. The motor is revving up. The plane vibrates, then begins to hum as it picks up speed on the runway. With one great shudder, we're airborne.

I like watching the airport get smaller below us and then seeing the tiny matchbook houses with swimming pools all lined up and the cars like ants moving on the crisscross of streets.

India is already tired of the window. She jams her head back against her head rest and closes her eyes. "What happens if she drives Uncle Red crazy? We'll be homeless," India says.

"She's not going to drive Uncle Red crazy," I tell her.

"Sure she is. She drives everyone crazy, except Dad because he never met her."

"Leave Dad out of this," I snap.

"I can talk about him whenever I want," India says. "You don't own him."

"India, just shut up, okay?" I tell her.

Mouse wiggles in her seat. "We're supposed to say our late father. Why, though? Was he late all the time?"

"Mouse, give it a rest," India says.

"I don't drive Bing crazy. Do I, Bing?" Mouse looks over as if he's seated in the aisle. She pauses for his answer. "He says no."

"Bing is made up, for the billionth time. He's all in your head." India snorts without opening her eyes.

"No, he's not. He has identification and everything. Do you want to see?"

"You drew his license. That's not real." India plugs in her headphones.

"No, there's something else I found when we were packing up but I'm not even going to show you," Mouse says.

India doesn't answer.

Mouse pulls off India's headphones and India goes ballistic. "I don't care. Do you hear me? I DO NOT CARE ABOUT ANYTHING YOU SAY, ANYTHING YOU SAW, ANYTHING YOU FOUND. Leave me alone!"

"Let up on her, okay? She's not the cause of every problem you have," I tell India.

"Yes, I am. I'm the cause of every problem she has," Mouse says proudly.

"Mouse, don't aggravate her."

"Maybe I'll have my own room. Actually, what I need is my own house," India announces.

"I need my own basketball court," I say.

"I need my own mouse wheel," Mouse says.

"If we are sharing a room, you are not getting mice." India puts her headphones back on.

46

Mouse organizes her markers all in a row and begins to draw. I've just settled in with one of the travel games my mom packed, a Rubik's Cube, when a bell goes off and the pilot comes over the speaker system. "Please return to your seats and fasten your seat belts. We've had reports of turbulence in our flight path. Flight attendants, please secure the cabin."

Bouncing, jerking all around. Turbulence is a polite term for this, that's for sure. It feels like the plane is having a seizure.

The sky outside looks strange; half dark, half light, as if somebody forgot to tell the day sky it was night and the two have met unexpectedly. India pulls the shade closed as the plane wobbles and dips.

A pretty flight attendant with puffy lips tries to maneuver the drink cart back down the aisle so she can buckle herself in. My stomach dives, then rises, bringing up the taste of leftover moo-shu pork.

Mouse keeps on coloring, undaunted by the bumps and vibrations. She is determined to finish copying a picture of a Black Hawk helicopter she found in the seat pouch. She put a dog in the pilot seat and another one riding on the tail of the helicopter.

"Henry?" I point to the brown dog. "But who's her friend?"

"Ask Henry," she answers as she begins drawing signs for the dog pilot. *No flying without dogs*, one says.

Mouse is having trouble with the second dog because the plane is jerking her markers all over the place. She

47

takes out the barf bag.

Uh-oh.

But no, she's not throwing up. She's trying to draw the helicopter on the barf bag. This is crazy, but at least she's quiet, at least she isn't scared, at least she's not trying to exit the plane and get her book again, and India isn't threatening to call the police. I think Mouse was just upset about not seeing Mom in the window. Sometimes when Mouse gets upset it comes out in a weird way. My mom told me that once.

Up, down, up, down. I'm thirsty, I want to get rid of the Chinese food taste in my mouth that's making my tongue feel hairy, but there's no way the flight attendant will be able to serve drinks now.

"India?" I flick the fringe on my sister's vest. "What's going on?" I've never been on a flight with this many bumps. "When is this going to end?"

She shrugs, not the least bit concerned. She is more upset that she can't text Maddy because you're not allowed to use your cell when the plane is in the air.

But hey wait. I push open the blind again. It looks as if we're landing. We hit the runway hard, the tires bump and hit, bump and hit like the ground has come up too soon.

My mom must have gotten these tickets cheap. Maybe pilot-in-training flights are half price because this pilot has no idea what he's doing. I'd have done a better job than him. At least we landed, though. Jeez.

I look over at India.

Her forehead has worry lines. She peeks at her cell. "It's only been an hour," she whispers in my ear.

"Time change?" I suggest. "Mom said it was an hour difference. Maybe your cell changes time zones automatically."

She nods hesitantly, then raises the window shade to peer at the sky. It's night now, except for this one patch of blue—a puzzle piece from the wrong puzzle.

"You should call Mom," I suggest. "Now that we're down, you're allowed."

She clicks open her cell and hits the home icon, listens for a minute, then shoves the phone in my ear. *The number you have reached has been disconnected,* the recorded message states.

We catch each other's eye. The home icon isn't home anymore.

India stares out into the black part of the night. She takes a deep breath and hits the icon for Mom's cell.

I hear my mom's recorded voice. At least her cell isn't disconnected.

India sighs and leaves a message: "Hi Mom." Her voice trembles. "We're here. The plane just landed. Call us, okay?"

Mouse stands up. She's finally finished copying the helicopter and she's ready to go.

"C'mon," she scolds. "We're the only ones left on the plane."

49

FINN

CHAPTER 7
BEYOND THE JETWAY

When I walk by the cockpit, the door is open and I see the pilot writing on his clipboard. From the back he definitely looks young. How old do you have to be to fly a commercial airline anyway?

My footsteps sound hollow on the Jetway rug as if there's nothing underneath us, but that's the way Jetways are. They aren't built to the ground on a solid foundation the way a building is. "India, what was it Mom told us we're supposed to do now?" I ask.

I steer my roller bag over the metal connector ridges with one arm and hold Mouse's hand with the other.

"She said somebody would be here to meet us in baggage claim. She said they'd have a sign," India reports.

"Uncle Red won't be meeting us?" I ask.

"What kind of sign?" Mouse hops up and down.

"He doesn't drive in Denver. He drives, but not that far, or not at night. I dunno, something like that. He sent some kind of car service." India is walking as if she has to think about each footstep.

"What kind of a sign?" Mouse is shouting now.

"One with our name on it," India explains impatiently.

"That's how we'll know to go with him," I say. "Remember how when we went to New York, there were people holding signs by the baggage claim?"

Mouse's legs are like springs. She can't walk normally when she gets excited. "Yeah, but it's not New York," she says.

"Duh, Mouse," India snaps as we move past the gate into the lonely terminal.

"Not Albuquerque. Not Phoenix. Not Salt Lake City. Not Ukiah." Mouse keeps bouncing up and thudding down. It must be pretty late or else Denver is a smaller city than I thought, but it's the capital of Colorado . . . isn't it? Why is the airport so quiet?

Mouse is still holding my hand, stretching my arm as far as it will go. She's peering intently at something.

"What is she doing?" India asks me.

I shrug. "C'mon, Mouse." I gently pull her along.

"Not Tucson. Not Las Vegas. Not Grand Junction," Mouse mumbles, bumping her suitcase behind her.

51

We're getting on one of those moving sidewalks. It's traveling through a long passageway with mostly blank walls, except now and then a mural. A flock of birds in the air on one side, herons in the marsh on the other. The usual airporty stuff—a cross between a doctor's waiting room and a tunnel.

The airport is dimly lit. A janitor is mopping the floor by one concession stand. Another stand has a roll-down metal curtain, drawn and locked. The man behind the cash register tosses change into his cash drawer, the coins clinking rhythmically with his count.

"India, what time is it?" I ask.

She gets her cell out again. "Now it says almost midnight. That doesn't make sense," she mumbles.

"Maybe it's wrong."

"Oh no . . . that's right," Mouse says. "That's what the man with the green socks said."

India rolls her eyes. "Whoever he is."

I look around at the deserted airport. "No one flies at night here?"

"Apparently not." India's voice doesn't have her usual bite to it. Her eyes are watchful.

I'm so busy trying not to think of all the bad things that could happen to three kids in an airport at night that I can hardly see straight. I took karate a few years ago, but I'm not even a yellow belt.

The moving sidewalk ends and we walk across a carpet that looks like a thousand birds with interlocking

52

wings and then another moving sidewalk begins. Where are we going to meet this guy with the sign? How long will it take to get to Uncle Red's?

Mouse looks beat. She'll probably fall asleep in the car. That doesn't sound like a bad idea to me either. I'm in no rush to get to Uncle Red's house. The only house I want to see is the one we left behind.

Another short moving sidewalk takes us to the baggage area and there up ahead leaning against a wall is a short guy holding a white board that says TOMPKINS in careful capital letters.

"Look! That's us!" Mouse points, hopping on one foot.

The man has a yellow vest, buttoned-down shirt, and gray suit pants but no jacket. He has a baby face with big bushy eyebrows, a thick mustache, and long sideburns, black like skid marks. He's wearing a taxi driver's cap that makes his ears stick out.

The driver smiles as he takes India's suitcase, sensing she's the one who would want princess treatment. Or maybe he thinks she's cute. I've had trouble with guys on my basketball team checking her out before. What do you do when the center on your team says your sister is hot? I'm hoping she gets a lot more zits or grows an arm out of the middle of her forehead really soon.

India's hand combs her long hair, holding it back as if she wants to put it in a ponytail. She can't like *him*, can she? This little man is peculiar, plus she's taller than he is.

"I'm parked thataway," the driver says, and we follow him across an almost deserted street.

The only vehicles on the airport road are Segways.

"Don't mind them," our driver says. "They're always here."

"Segway riders?" I ask.

"Yep. They're waiting for flights that won't ever arrive."

"Why not?"

"Not on the schedule."

I'm trying to make sense of this as Mouse twists my arm like taffy. "It's going to be a limo. I know it."

But the car is a shocking pink taxi with silky white feathers stuck to it in even rows as if someone had spent the better part of a month with a glue stick and a bag of feathers, carefully laying them end to end. It has bright pink whitewall tires and a pearlescent license plate that says WHTBIRD. It's the kind of car you might see down by the boardwalk at Venice Beach where the kooks all live.

This can't be the taxi, limo, whatever. We shouldn't get in this car.

Mouse has a funny look on her face, as if she's found a hair in her hamburger. She hangs back with me, but India doesn't seem worried.

"Cool," she says, snapping shots with her cell phone. She smiles at the little man as if this isn't the slightest bit odd. The little man clicks his keys, and the feathers all rotate outward. The door opens automatically, revealing lush pink upholstery inside.

Mouse's lips pucker uncertainly. "Bing is not sure this is safe," she whispers.

"Just who I wanted to take a safety lesson from . . ." India snorts. "Bing."

"India, Mouse is right. This is too weird," I whisper. "You need to call Mom."

India raises an eyebrow, but she clicks open her cell phone and pushes Mom's icon, a bright red teacher's apple. Once again, the call goes directly to Mom's recorded message.

She clicks the cell closed. "Does it look like we have a lot of options here?" she asks.

The airport is eerie at night. The usual traveling hustle and bustle is completely missing. It's cold and dark, and I'm exhausted. The soft plush taxi seats and the warm glow of the light inside beckons to us. There's something that doesn't quite add up about the driver, but he has a nice smile—clearly genuine.

"It's an unusual vehicle," he concedes.

"Uncle Red would have chosen a good taxi service. And Mom trusts Uncle Red, otherwise we wouldn't be going to live with him," India announces, but even she sounds doubtful.

"Bing thinks we should call Uncle Red," Mouse announces.

"Now there's an idea," I say.

India grinds her teeth, but she pops open her cell and dials the number Mom made her program in for Uncle Red.

Mouse and I move in close to hear what Uncle Red has to say, but Uncle Red's phone is a fast busy signal, which means the call isn't going through.

India and I look at each other.

"Would you prefer to stay here?" the little man asks gently. The car is weird, but the guy couldn't be nicer. I trust him, I don't know why.

"He did have our name. How else would he have our name if Uncle Red didn't give it to him?" I offer.

Our suitcases are already loaded in the trunk. They fit perfectly too—as if the trunk was custom-made for three roller bags.

"Okay," India says to the driver. "We'll go with you." She tosses her hair back over her shoulder and gets in.

Mouse's bright blue eyes are half hidden by her red lashes in a strange un-Mouse-like way.

"You okay with this, Mouse?" I ask.

Mouse's little chest heaves, like she's hyperventilating. "Will Bing get to sit in the front?" she asks, digging Bing's wallet out of her suitcase. She opens it and flashes her handmade ID.

The driver nods as if this makes perfect sense to him and opens the front passenger-side door, then closes it again, presumably after Bing is inside.

The car looks so comfortable I can hardly wait to

56

climb in. I scoot into the backseat after India. Mouse follows me.

When we're all buckled in—including Bing, Mouse insists on this—the feather taxi glides out of the dark airport parking lot, along the mostly deserted streets.

What I notice first is how comfortable the backseat is. It doesn't even feel as if the tires are making contact with the road. It's more like they're hovering over rather than rolling on the street.

When we reach the open highway, there are mountains everywhere, beautiful mountains with snowcapped peaks. At the foot of the mountains is a bright, shiny lake glistening like a mirrored welcome mat. Through the skylight you can see how bright the stars are. The scenery is spectacular. My mom was right about that. Who knows . . . maybe she'll be right about Uncle Red too.

On the dashboard is a brass plate engraved with *Property of FB*. *FB* must be Fort Baker. On the sun visor is the taxi driver's name. *Charles,* it says. I can see India reading it too. "So." India clears her throat. "Um, Charles. You know the address. Uncle Red already gave it to you, right?"

Charles takes the radio—it's an old-fashioned kind that fits neatly in the palm of his hand, like the sort taxi driver dispatchers in movies have, except it's attached by a pink curly cord to the dashboard. He mutters into the microphone, then he turns back to us. "You can call me Chuck," he says in a high, sweet voice.

India and I look at each other. She seems to be thinking what I'm thinking. Inside the cab, we can hear Chuck much more clearly. His voice has brought him in focus. I lean forward to inspect his sideburns and mustache. They're fake, glued right on. Chuck isn't a short man, he's a kid.

"Um, Chuck, we want a real taxi, okay?" My voice is pinched. "We need an adult driving."

"Yes, well, driving is a kid's job," Chuck observes.

India snorts. "Is that so?" she asks.

"That's the way it is here, yes," Chuck answers politely.

I peer out the window, looking for a sign. "Where is here? Fort Baker or Denver?"

Chuck shakes his head. He seems genuinely apologetic. "Always happens. Can't ever get the signage just right. People think this is Portland or Chicago. Dallas or New Orleans. We put up as many signs as we can, but . . ."

"What signs?"

"The ones I've been telling you about. The ones that said: *Not Albuquerque. Not Las Vegas. Not Denver,*" Mouse pipes up.

"Trouble is there's so many places this isn't, it's hard to cover them all. Just yesterday we had someone from Duluth." He sighs. "You know, there isn't a single sign that says *Not Duluth.*"

"Why do you have signs that say what this isn't?" India asks.

"It's the first comment passengers always make."

Chuck lowers his voice in imitation of an older man. "'Hey um, sir, this isn't Cleveland?'"

"Okay," I say. "But if it's not any of those places, where is it?"

"We're headed for Falling Bird. It's beautiful, isn't it? The sky is a color you don't often see." We look up at the luminous midnight blue sky, glistening with stars like a thousand glittering pencil points. "Sometimes there's a little patch of day sky, then you know it's a special night. I saw one earlier. It's probably gone by now. You got to catch them quick," Chuck explains.

"Like a shooting star?" Mouse asks, her voice sleepy.

"Exactly," Chuck agrees.

"Falling Bird must be on the way to Fort Baker. You know Uncle Red's address? Red Tompkins? He lives near the Horsehair reservoir. That's where we're going, right?" India is leaning forward, straining against her seat belt, which rubs the feathers off. They fall gently to the floor.

Chuck shrugs. "I never met Uncle Red," he admits.

I shoot India a wary look.

"Uncle Red called the taxi. He wouldn't have met him," India whispers.

I know she's right, but even so. This is all a little odd. "Maybe you should take us back to the airport," I suggest.

"Okay, but I'm not sure you're going to want to stay at the airport."

"Why not?" I ask.

59

"No flights out from there."

"But it's an airport," I insist.

"He means this late," India says.

"Did you get our name from Uncle Red?" I ask.

"Sparky told me," Chuck says. "He runs the information group and he teaches Century Awareness."

"What's Sensory Awareness?" I ask.

"Century, not sensory. We call it CA. It just means keeping up with things. If you have contact with passengers, you need to know what's happening."

Mouse's head nestles against my arm. Poor kid is even more exhausted than I am. She's already asleep. "So this Sparky guy radios you with names of passengers on the flight."

"Yes, I believe you were on flight number two-eighty-eight."

"That's right," India says.

This isn't making much sense, but the logic seems less and less important "Where is everybody else?" I ask, sinking back into the soft seats, a warm contentment flowing over me.

"I only had room for you," Chuck explains, his words as slow as syrup.

"Oh," I say, comforted by this answer despite how puzzling it is. Of course he didn't have room for the entire plane full of people in this one cab. What is he talking about?

"Then where are we going?" India asks as she too falls back into the weightless warmth of the seats.

"You'll see. It's pretty amazing. Like nothing you've ever experienced before."

My mind is still firing questions, but the rest of me feels as if it's been submerged in warm bathwater. "India, we need to go home."

"Got to get you to your new home," Chuck says as the feather taxi increases speed, gliding along in the dark valley with a new set of mountain peaks off in the distance.

I struggle to find my normal thoughts. It feels as if I've been wrapped in heated velvet. "Let's call Mom again," I suggest.

"You know, our technology has some gaps. We haven't had anybody with a good grasp of cellophones arrive yet."

"Cell phones," I correct.

"Cell phones. Shoot. Don't tell Sparky about that, okay?"

"Let's try calling," I insist, struggling to hold on to these words before they dissolve like sugar in the warm puddle of my mind.

India unzips her vest pocket slowly, as if each tooth of the zipper is a note she can't wait to hear. She flips open her cell and stares at it, mesmerized. Her finger wavers above the icons before it finally makes contact with my mom's red apple.

We wait, the car purring along the highway in the strange dark night.

"Dead?" Chuck asks after a time, though I don't

know how long. I had forgotten we were waiting.

India nods. "Maybe closer to the city," she suggests.

Chuck shakes his head. "Won't help. Once you're out of the area the calls get dropped."

Won't help . . . out of the area . . . his words echo through my head, through my sleep, through my dreams. The calls get dropped . . . dropped . . . dropped.

CHAPTER 8
TRAVELS WITH CHUCK

Bing says it's time to wake up, but I fall asleep again. I can't do everything Bing says, you know. India is bossy enough.

I think we've only been sleeping a few hours, but it's late morning already and we are still in the car with feathers. When are we going to get to Uncle Red's?

India and Finn are asleep. India has her head by the door, her hair stuck with spit to her mouth. Finn is curled up on the seat. He looks like a comma. I check to see if he has grown any pimples overnight. None. Good.

Bing is already up. That is the nice thing about an invisible friend, he is always up before me. I never have to be even one minute without him. I'm always his favorite person too. I'm no one else's favorite person. Pluto probably wasn't either, so they kicked him out of the solar system. I hope they don't kick me out of the solar system. I watch for signs that say *Not the Solar System,* but I don't see any.

Bing is chatty this morning. Usually he doesn't notice other people that much, but he says Mr. Chuck is a good guy and we should trust him. I spy on Mr. Chuck, but he doesn't do anything interesting. He just drives. That's all.

"How come you get to drive?" I ask.

I see Chuck's dimples in the rearview mirror. He's taken off his jacket, which says *Travels with Charles* in thread above the pocket. "Good morning, Mouse. I was just about to wake you up."

"How come you don't need a driver's license?"

"I have one," Chuck says.

"Does it have a picture on it?"

"Yes."

"How old are you?"

"Twelve."

"You can't get a driver's license when you're twelve, otherwise Finn and India would have them."

"Things are different here."

"Yeah, I know. My mom doesn't have the right teaching credenza," I say.

"That's too bad. I would have liked to have met her," Chuck says, and then points up through the windshield. "Mouse, look up in the sky. Over on the left there."

In the bright blue sky there are no clouds, but in big white writing it says: *Welcome, Mouse*. I can read it even though it's cursive. I don't like to read cursive as much, though. They never put cursive in books, and I'm glad about that.

"How'd they know I was coming?" I ask.

"Everybody knows you're coming."

"Does the president know?"

"Of course. Now wake your sister and brother. They won't want to miss this."

"India! In-deee-aaa!!" I jiggle the leather fringe on her vest, which she tells me never to pull on or she will hang me upside down out the window when we are driving on the freeway after she gets her license and she can finally drive. "My name is in the sky! The president knows!"

She jerks upright and scrunches her face like she can't pull her eyes out of her dreams. "Huh?"

I point to the sky outside the window.

Finn is awake now too. He's not a comma anymore. He's back to being straight like an exclamation point. "What the heck? India! Your name's in the sky!"

"*My* name?" India is really interested now.

"There." Finn points and India and I scootch over until we see *Welcome, India*.

"Me too! Me too!" I tell Finn, pointing to my name. "Uh-oh." I lean forward to whisper to Chuck. "What about Finn? You forgot about him."

"He's up ahead," Chuck says, and then a minute later

we see *Welcome, Finn Tompkins* out the front window just as the *W* in *Welcome, Mouse* is beginning to droop.

"How come Finn gets his last name too?" I ask.

"Because people need to know Finn's last name," Chuck answers.

Finn makes a funny gulp. Finn likes to write his whole name on things. I don't know why.

"How'd it get up there? Is there some computer program that does that?" I ask.

"No, we just have planes," Mr. Chuck explains. "We've got every kind of pilot here, lots of skywriters. Look what we're passing now."

A big shiny truck and a giant trailer are up ahead. Painted on the side of the trailer is a huge heart. Chuck pushes the feather taxi faster, and we practically fly by. The side of the truck says: *We love India, Finn, and Mouse.*

"The truck loves us?" I ask.

Chuck smiles. "Everybody loves you today. This is the best part of my job."

"How could the trucking company know in time to get the trucks painted?" Finn wants to know.

"Sparky is in charge of information. And then Francine and Mary Carol are good at coordinating. Together the three of them can do anything. Sparky and Francine don't get along that well, though," Chuck says.

We're approaching a city now—a beautiful city that's all sparkly white and silver with color streaming out of it like the prism in my classroom.

"Is that Denver?" India asks.

"No, it's *Not Denver*, remember?" I say.

"That's Falling Bird," Chuck says.

"FB is for Fort Baker, isn't it Mr. Chuck? Isn't it?" I say.

"FB stands for Fort Baker but in this case it means Falling Bird," Chuck tells me.

"How far is it from Falling Bird to Fort Baker?" Finn asks.

"It's a bit of a detour I'm afraid," Chuck says.

"Wait, does Uncle Red know about the detour?" India asks.

"Yes," Mr. Chuck says.

The road is full of cars now and each has a sign in the window. *Welcome, India. You are so beautiful. Sing for us*, one says. *Mouse is our favorite*, another says. *Finn rules.* And then *Ask Mouse. She knows everything. So does Bing.*

"But, Mr. Chuck, how do they know Bing? He didn't have a real seat on the plane. And I've never told Uncle Red about him."

"Like I said, Sparky doesn't miss a thing," Mr. Chuck says.

I wish he would slow down. I want to say hello to the people who think I know everything. Bing does too. He thinks I know everything—except what he knows. We are side-by-side refrigerators full of knowing, Bing and me.

We are driving under a big Welcome to Falling Bird arch now. It is made of prisms and light. *Welcome to*

Falling Bird is written in pink light on the road. On the sidewalks are people waving to us. When we drive up, they all cheer.

"How could Sparky have told all these people?" I ask India.

"Did you post this online?" Finn wants to know.

"Uncle Red must have arranged this," India offers.

"Is Uncle Red rich?" Finn asks.

"He must be," India says.

"He sure knows a lot of people," I say, reading all the signs. *We love Mouse. Yay for India.* Some have mouse noses and ears. Some are dressed as basketball players. *MVP Finn Tompkins,* one guy's basketball shirt says. Every guy has the number 48. Finn's basketball number.

"Why are they carrying pictures of Henry?" Finn asks.

"She's your dog," Chuck says.

"How'd they know her name and what she looks like?" Finn again.

"Henry is important to you, so of course we'd know about her."

"How far are we from Uncle Red's?" Finn asks.

"*That* I don't know," Chuck answers.

"You need to take us back to the airport," Finn insists.

"If Uncle Red arranged all this, then it must be okay," India says.

Each light post is a bird nest with bulbs that are eggs. Feathers fall out of the sky. Pictures of a dark blue night sky with one piece of day sky are all around and movies are everywhere . . . on the roofs, on the sidewalks, on the tree tops, and even in some windows. People in Falling Bird must really like movies. And guess what? We're in them!

There's India doing cartwheels with Maddy, India singing in the choir, Finn shooting baskets with our cousins watching, Finn and Henry on Finn's bed, me explaining decimals to fifth graders, me riding horses with Mommy.

"Our life is up there," I say.

Chuck smiles. "We know how to make you feel welcome."

So many people are watching—too many to count, even the fast way where you multiply one side by the other. People don't stand in rows unless they are in a marching band or the army.

Chuck parks the feather cab under a shady tree full of pink flowers. Everybody watches the sky boards. We hear them oohh and ahhh and clap. It's like when I was student of the week . . . only better.

After a few minutes, the same movies begin again and Chuck drives back onto the driving part of the road. The cars and buses and carts all honk and flash their lights like we are famous. Chuck turns on to a street with big homes, and parks in the front yard of one. People on both sides shout our names. He takes off his cap and his mustache and puts them in his hat.

"Are they itchy?" I ask.

He shrugs. "I just wear them because they make my passengers feel more comfortable when I pick them up," Chuck says. "Now." He leans over the seat. "I need to tell you a few things. This is important, okay?" Chuck has messy hair that looks like he needs his mommy to cut it for him. He is nice. Bing is right about that.

"When you're done, I'm available to take you wherever you want to go as long as it's within your time, unless, of course, another flight comes in. And then I have to meet that one."

"Couldn't you take us to Uncle Red's now?" Finn asks as the crowd outside sings "Tomp-kins! Tomp-kins!"

"But if Uncle Red arranged all this, we can't refuse to do it. It will hurt his feelings," India insists.

"Tomp-kins! Tomp-kins!" People keep saying our name!

"You won't want to miss this, trust me. It's the most incredible experience of your life. Just keep your eye on the time, because it will be different for each of you. That's the first thing to remember."

"Excuse me, Mr. Chuck, the time is the same for everybody. Three o'clock for me is three o'clock for you." Kids get confused sometimes, so I have to explain things to them.

Chuck puts his hands up. "Just try to follow, okay? Each of you is an individual and you have your own personal time."

"I'm not confused. It's you that's confused, Mr. Chuck," I tell him.

"Wait . . . why are you saying this? You're not going to leave us . . . are you?" Finn asks.

"I'm afraid so. Now second thing, if you want me *after,* just call. But it has to be all three of you. They won't let me come for just one. Bit of a vehicle shortage, I'm afraid. Carpooling is encouraged here."

"After *what?*" Finn asks.

"Of course it would be all three of us, Mr. Chuck, sir," I tell him. "My mom said India has to stay with us, and Finn is always here."

India crosses her arms. "Look, you can't just leave us."

Chuck unrolls the windows. He tips his head toward the people shouting "Tomp-kins! Tomp-kins!"

"Listen to that," Chuck says. He has the doors open and the feathers up. He must have an open-all-the-seat-belts button, because I did not touch mine and it's unbuckled.

"If we want you after what?" Finn insists.

"Yeah, after *what,* Mr. Chuck?" I ask.

"Wait." India buckles her seat belt again. "How will we call you? You said the cell didn't work here. And anyway, I don't have your number."

Chuck smiles the nice smile with the dimples. "Thanks, India. I almost forgot. Here." He gives a piece of wood to each of us. "Put the pieces together and I will be there."

I turn the wood over in my hand. It's carved with one leaf growing from a small branch at the top. It smells of trees. Each one looks like this, only different.

It's a puzzle. But before I can put it together, we are out of the car, only I never told my arms or legs to get out. It isn't a bumpy getting-out-of-the-car either. It's smooth like when Mommy puts my honey in the microwave. I put the piece of wood in my pocket and grab my blue roller bag.

The air smells like flowers, dirt, and peanut butter cookies. Every step is springy like my feet are bouncing balls. People sing our names. My name makes a beautiful song. Almost as nice as Bing's.

"Look! See! The Tompkins three," people chant as Chuck waves good-bye.

My feet know where they're going. I want to ask Bing how that's possible, but he's busy looking at everything. My feet walk me up a sidewalk made of smooth flat stones. The walk splits into three paths. Between the white stones are gray stones that make a giant M for Mouse and a small B for Bing. There is an F for Finn on Finn's path and I for India on the end one.

The paths lead to big homes like on TV. India's is teenagery sparkly with gold hangy things and a rug with India's name in bright letters. There are round pink, lime green, and orange lights and a polka-dot carpet inside the open door. A fluffy white cat sits on the window seat.

Finn's home is made of wood with a gray stone chimney. It has big windows and trees all around. It is an olden day's house that smells like a fireplace and looks like a bear might visit soon. On the side is a basketball court with a real scoreboard and places for Mommy and me to sit and watch Finn.

Finn is staring at his house with his mouth open like at the dentist. India is walking up her sidewalk.

My home is yellow with white trim, a porch swing, pots with flowers, and clouds of butterflies and hummingbirds and fireflies everywhere. It is glowy with yellow light. My house is better than Finn's or India's.

In the doorway is a lady with red curly hair like mine. She has a science book in one hand, a plate of peanut butter–chocolate chip cookies in the other. I can smell them. That's how I know. "'Pluto,'" she reads, "'is the ninth planet in the solar system.'"

I don't know who this stranger person is. She isn't like my mommy at all. This mommy is better.

INDIA

CHAPTER 9
A COOL MOM

Okay, I have no idea how we got these incredible houses and everything. It had to have been Uncle Red, right? He must have like pulled some strings somehow. Too bad Mom can't see how well Uncle Red and I are taking care of Finn and Mouse. I mean hello? Look at this! I'll bet Uncle Red didn't have to work his butt off or freak out about it either. Life is a lot easier than Mom makes it out to be.

There's a group of girls about my age pointing at me from the sidewalk.

I have fans . . . who knew?

Why didn't I read the celebrity magazines Maddy always buys? Then I'd know what you're supposed to say to fans. Fans love you no matter what, don't they? I'll bet that's what Maddy would say.

Maddy understands things way better than Mom. I just wish she were here right now, because I'm feeling a little clueless about what I'm supposed to do.

I feel bad I didn't tell Maddy I was moving. I didn't even say good-bye. What if they put up a sign that says the house has been repoed, foreclosed, sold by the bank, whatever . . . and what if Maddy sees it?

They won't do that, right?

Maddy would freak if she saw this place. This house is awesome. It's ten times nicer than Lizzie's house. I wish I could tell her how to get here. There's a number 401 next to the door, but what street?

How did it work that I got this place? I mean, if Uncle Red arranged it, wouldn't he be here? That's the part I don't get.

But maybe Uncle Red wants us to enjoy this without him. When he sends a gift for my birthday, it's not like he flies in to give it to me.

Maddy says when something good happens, don't question it. Just go for it.

I need a clean set of clothes that aren't, you know, slept in. What should I wear though? How do you dress if you're a celebrity?

I'm just unzipping my suitcase, digging through looking for my turquoise skirt, when this lady comes out who kinda looks like my mom, only much younger, much cooler, much more fun; my mom without the worry.

"In—" The mom-like person smiles at me. "You're not going to believe this," she says, leading me through this incredible, foyer kind of place to a room bigger than our living room, full of new clothes.

"Here you go, girl," the lady says. "I'll leave you to it."

The first thing I see are plum-colored pants like the ones Maddy has that I've been dying for but my mom says are too expensive. And ohmygod tons of boyfriend jeans, hundreds of shoes, and boots—real ones, not the knockoffs I always have to wear.

Seriously expensive tops too—long sleek ones that make you look skinny and tall. There must be a hundred, hanging up like in a cool boutique, and then there are whole outfits accessorized in really cute ways. Everything is my style. Better than my style. The me I've always wanted to be. Nobody can pick out what I like all the time, but this woman has. If only Maddy or Ariana or even Lizzie were here. We would have a blast trying things on.

I slip into the plum-colored pants like Maddy's. They are so cute and they fit perfectly. I can't believe the way I look in this stuff. Ten times better than normal. Even my birthmark looks great here, like my belly would not look right without it. Isn't that crazy? I always thought it looked like mud, but here it resembles a bird in flight.

Then I drift past the closet room to another room—even bigger than the last. Inside are dozens of screens and photos of Maddy and her friends. But they are all static photo faces, except Maddy's.

Maddy's hand beckons in that rapid-fire way she has. "In, come closer! Oh my God, what are you wearing? That top is too cute."

"You think?" I turn so she can see the back, which is the most adorable part because of the way it's cut low.

"Get out of here, girl! That is adorable! You better hide that one from Rules. She'd never let you wear anything like that. Has Brendan seen it? Is he on screen? Have you talked to him yet?" Maddy whispers in her throaty voice.

I look over at his photo. How could I talk to him? He's just a photo of himself. Maybe there's a texting component. Maddy would totally know about that and she'd expect me to know too. "No," I say.

"Well, go say hello. Just, you know, walk by his screen."

"Just walk by? How weird is that?"

"Like he hasn't checked you out already? Wait, don't turn around. He's watching now, I can kinda see."

How can I ever leave Maddy? And Brendan? I can't believe he likes me, but Maddy swears he does and she would know.

I look around for the mom-like person. Rules would be all over me for this. The second I'm having fun, she comes up with some new rule that puts an end to it.

This woman is cool. She knows when to show up and when to fade away. She comes back in just as I'm looking for her.

"You want to look around now?" she asks. She's wearing this gold ring with a killer stone in it. It looks totally real. As soon as she sees my eyes on it, she says, "You want to borrow the ring?"

"Are you sure it's okay?" I ask.

"Of course," she says. "I don't care about stuff like that."

I put it on. It looks totally great, but it makes me uncomfortable.

"It's okay really, In," she says. "I know what happened with Maddy . . ."

"Maddy would never in a million years steal anything," I tell her. "She just borrowed it."

"I know," she says.

Still, I give her ring back. I've had enough of rings for my whole entire life.

This house is unbelievable—it's so clean, for one thing. It's as if Ariana's neurotic mom ran around here with her vacuum. At our house I'm the maid. Finn is supposed to do the yard and the wash. But c'mon, the yard is the size of a teaspoon and all he has to do is put the clothes in the machine. How hard is that? Whereas I scrub the floors like I'm Cinderella. Thank God none of my friends ever saw that.

Here there isn't just one living room and one bathroom either. There are gobs of living rooms and dozens of bathrooms; huge ones with makeup and lip gloss in a zillion colors and big cases of eye shadows like they have at the cosmetics counter of department stores.

My mom won't even let me wear makeup. How ridiculous is that? But thinking of my mom makes me realize she'll kill me if I forget to check on Finn and Mouse.

The second this thought occurs to me, the woman pushes a button and a gigantic screen pulls down from the ceiling. On it I see Mouse in a room painted to look like the night sky. She is busy hanging planets.

The mom person she's with looks just like her. The woman appears to be enjoying herself too. Must be a great actress, because she's got to be sick to death of Mouse by now. Mouse tires everyone out—even the nice people.

Mom thinks Finn helps with Mouse, but I'm the one with all the responsibility. I'm the one who has to share a room with her and give her a bath and let her borrow my underwear.

The second I think of Finn, the screen shimmers to a new scene: Finn and his dad person playing ball. His dad person gives Finn a thumbs-up. Finn smiles. You can totally see him too. He's not hiding behind his hair.

I follow my cool mom into the kitchen, which has three refrigerators stuffed full of Cokes and root beers. On the stove, a pan of cinnamon buns and a boysenberry pie are cooling. My real mom never has time to bake unless it's for Finn or Mouse.

I sink my teeth into a warm cinnamon bun and get a rush of buttery, cinnamony flavor. I pour myself a hot chocolate, grab a bag of chips, and head for the library. My real mom likes books, so we went to the library a lot when I was little. But this place is more like a bookstore. Every book is brand-new—the kind of books you have to wait for months to get from the library.

It's full of light and window seats and snuggly pillows and fish—ohmygod, a wall-size aquarium full of fish—and one white cat stalking.

Stupid cat . . . what's it doing here? Then I remember I saw a white cat I wanted once. That's freaky. How could anyone know that? I never even told Maddy.

My cool mom seems to guess what I'm thinking. "I pay attention," she says as the cat eyes me like I'm a frenemy.

"No kidding," I say. "I'm not used to it."

"Your mom's busy."

"She always has time for Finn and Mouse."

My cool mom's head doesn't move, but her eyes register that she knows I'm right. "She thinks you're older."

"She doesn't care about what's important to me."

My cool mom nods. "Your dad was the people guy. You're more like him. You scare your mom. She doesn't know how to protect you where you're going," she tells me as she reaches down to stroke the white kitty, who is purring loudly like she needs a cat-sized muffler.

I find another screen and check to see if Mouse is driving her mom person nuts yet. She's just built a gigantic volcano with a remote control device that sends hot lava spewing out a hole in the roof. Now she's walking to her bedroom, which is a room-size climbing structure next to a condo for mice. I mean check this out: fifteen tiny bedrooms with tiny mice asleep in tiny beds, their tiny bedside lamps turned off. Mouse climbs up to her bed high in the tree house.

"The higher you go, the safer you'll be. Remember that . . . it's important," her mom person tells her.

That makes no sense. The higher up you go, the farther you'll fall down. I guess her mom person is a little off, just like Mouse. Whatever.

Not to worry. It looks safe up there—the bed has tall slat sides, so she won't fall out. My real mom would kill me if Mouse got hurt.

Mouse curls up under the branches, then her mom person strokes her cheek and sings softly, "B-I-N-G, B-I-N-G, B-I-N-G, and Bingo was his name-o."

At night when she's asleep, Mouse is kind of sweet. Then in the morning she's like a pop-up you can't get rid of.

Finn's room has a big tent, with a little tent inside it. His name is on everything. The sheets, the pillows, the bookshelf, the tent, the canvas walls. Even the dog collars say: *Property of Finn Tompkins.* I don't see him, though. He's probably already inside the tent sound asleep.

I'm beat too, so I head for my bed that has a million pillows with polka dots and zigzags and checkerboard squares in all shapes and sizes.

I sink into my comforter with my new cool clothes on. There are a bazillion pairs of pajamas, but I'm too tired to decide which to wear. The bed is so soft it's like diving into a down feather swimming pool. I don't worry that I'm going to bed at three a.m. I can sleep late in the morning. My cool mom will know that about me.

As I'm falling asleep, I think about what I will wear tomorrow. The gray pants with the purple and pink shirt that makes my stomach look so flat. Or that like short, flouncy skirt with the brown sweater that's so soft it feels like lamb's ears. And what will I eat for breakfast? I know . . . Belgian waffles with whipped cream, fresh blueberries, and hot chocolate. Everything about this place is incredible!

CHAPTER 10
COURTESY PHONE

Who wouldn't love this house? It's like a cabin in the woods—with chairs made of branches, thick rugs, high ceilings, and a big old-fashioned stone fireplace. There are also these buttons with symbols on the wall. I touch one and a different room appears. When I push the basketball button, the indoor court comes to me. The fireplace room is in the center of the house and it stays still while the other rooms revolve on tracks around it.

I push the kitchen button because I'm starving. When the kitchen arrives, this guy appears. He looks like my dad, with freckles, curly red hair, and bushy red eyebrows. His voice is different, his face is rounder, and he's taller, but there's clearly a resemblance. It's as if someone studied a photo of my dad and then found a look-alike.

This dad look-alike guy brings me a Philly cheese steak sandwich, onion rings, and soda. I dig in.

"How'd you know I like Philly cheese steak?" I ask between bites.

"This is your dream house. Of course we'll stock it with your favorite foods."

"But how did you know what they are?"

"Sparky told me."

"Sparky again."

He nods. "Look Finn, just take it on face value. If you think too much, worry about every little thing, you'll get in your own way."

"How will I get in my own way?"

"You'll lose time."

"That doesn't make sense."

"Sure it does. If you spend all your time worrying about the future, you can't enjoy the present." He takes a deep breath and starts again. "This time in your house is for you to enjoy. You need it to prepare you for your journey."

"To Uncle Red's?"

"If that's where you want to go."

"What if it isn't?"

He shrugs. "You'll have to consider other options."

What are my other options? I wonder. Going to live with Aunt Sammy and Uncle Tito? Mom said that wasn't possible. Apparently I don't have any other options. I'm not going to say that. I don't want this guy to think I'm a loser with no place to go.

"Ready for pie?" he asks. He seems to understand I want to drop the subject.

"Yes," I say as a screen in the back of the kitchen goes live with a movie clip of a basketball game I played in. Coach P. is giving me instructions from the sidelines like I'm one of his starting guys. That only happened once, but it was the best game of my life!

Without me saying anything, my dad look-alike replays it over and over again.

I'm not sure how many times I watch, before I finally pull myself away. Then we play basketball one on one until it gets dark. On the way inside I thank him for everything, then explain it's time to go home.

"Home?" he asks.

"To Uncle Red's then," I whisper miserably.

"You're sure?"

"Look, Mr. Whatever-Your-Name-Is. I need to know what's going on here."

He smiles at this as if I've just given the answer to a difficult question. Together we walk to the center fireplace room, where he pushes a small button with a question mark. Within seconds a loudspeaker blares overhead. "Finn Tompkins, please step to the white courtesy phone. Finn Tompkins, white courtesy phone."

I head for the wall, pick out the icon with the white phone, and press it. As soon as it lights up, the court moves off on its track and a new room arrives. This room is small with a simple wooden alcove and a comfortable overstuffed armchair. In front of the chair is a white phone with no buttons, just a smooth dial-less face.

"Finn Tompkins . . . the white courtesy phone," the loudspeaker voice urges.

I pick up the phone. "Hello?"

"Finn Tompkins?" the computerized voice asks.

"Yes."

"Sparky would like to see you."

CHAPTER 11
INDIA'S CAT

'm used to knowing more than everyone else on account of Bing. He has in some knee-a, you know. You can find out a lot of things when you're awake at night.

In the morning Bing tells me what he learned the night before.

Sometimes he wakes me up so I can hear too. Once I heard Mommy on the phone. She said she didn't know if Maddy was the worst thing to happen to India or the best.

She should have asked me. I know all about Maddy. She stole Mommy's engagement ring. Mommy says I could have been "mistaken" and I'm supposed to stop talking about this, but Bing is never mistaken. Maddy and

India were doing homework on the computer, and India went to make popcorn, which is the only food Maddy will eat at our house on account of Mommy won't buy junk food.

While India was gone, Maddy opened Mommy's jewelry box. She took the ring out.

The next week Mommy said her engagement ring was gone.

Mommy said maybe Maddy put it back when I didn't see. But then why was it gone after that? Mommy talked to Maddy and Maddy's mom about it. Maddy's mom said I was "a fanciful child."

Maddy has another name for me. She calls me Demon Child.

Mommy got her ring back after that. A few weeks later it appeared in her jewelry box again. Then Mommy told India and me we aren't allowed to talk about it anymore. We just hate each other in the quiet now.

Bing got more facts about Falling Bird too. He found out that this mom lady is a rental. He thinks there are rental dads and rental dogs too. Bing said it will be hard for India to leave Falling Bird. He also said her cat doesn't like her very much. Bing said Finn is figuring out how the whole place works. Finn has to know stuff. He's like me!

Bing said it wasn't so bad here. It was fun to see all the good things about his life on the big screen.

He said we might want to stay.

But I don't want to change moms for good.

INDIA

CHAPTER 12
THE RUMBLING

When I wake up, the sun is shining through the window, and I can smell waffles and hot chocolate. I stay tucked into the soft sheets, basking in the coziness, until my cool mom comes in.

"Good morning, India. Did you sleep okay?" she asks.

I don't answer. I don't have to. My cool mom totally gets how I feel. She doesn't say much and she hasn't mentioned one single rule either. Moms are okay when they keep their mouths shut. My cool mom gets stuff like this. She totally does.

"It's been great getting to know you," she says. "I like how enthusiastic you are about everything."

"Really? My real mom says I have a bad attitude and I'm not enthusiastic about anything."

"You just like different things than she does."

"How do you know me so well?"

"Sparky gives us a lot of information. And I kind of get you. You remind me of me when I was your age."

I scoot myself up, propping my back with the biggest pillow like we're going to have a girlfriend talk—the kind I never have with my real mom.

But a rumbling begins low in the building like somebody turned on a forced air heater down on the first floor. It's a slight vibration that builds to a shaking motion as if I'm standing next to the tracks when a train flies by.

"What is that?" I ask as the bed begins to rock like a cradle, but I'm not a baby and I don't like it.

A tree limb cracks outside the window.

My cool mom is standing with a stupid expression on her face waving good-bye. Good-bye? Where is she going?

"Hey!" I scream as the splintering grows louder and the bed begins to split apart in a jagged line down the middle.

"Help!" I shriek as I try to get a grip on the slipping, sliding bed covers. I grab the side of the bed, the wall, the pillow, something permanent, but it all slides through my fingers. Everything is in motion.

Why doesn't my cool mom do something?

She's standing there watching, twiddling her fingers

in a twinkling wave, as my whole body gets sucked down through darkness, a black hole, a tunnel. My hand hits the side, bends my fingers back, my ankle bone bonks the wall, and a sharp pain pierces my foot as I speed downward unable to stop myself.

Instinctively I roll up in a cannonball, my arms protecting my head. Now I'm spinning faster and faster. My legs are tucked tightly, I'm gripping my ankles. I can't see anything but endless black and black and black as I hurl down. Ohmygod maybe I'm blind. I will get sunglasses. I want to be the kind of blind person who wears sunglasses, I think as I spin down and down, until at last I see a perfect circle of light that slowly grows. My world flashes light for one blinding second, before I hit hard.

CHAPTER 13
AN ELEVATOR UP

Before I leave my dream home, my dad guy has me sign a stack of papers. Each page says more or less the same thing. *I, Finn Tompkins, understand under the laws of fair trade that I will be giving up time for information.* I remember my mom said when you buy a house it feels like you're signing your life away. But I'm not buying a house, so I don't understand the need for this. The dad guy just says that's the way they do things here.

When I'm finally finished, I arrange with him to get word to Mouse and India that I'll meet them later. Then I push the tram icon and the rooms rotate until the station appears. *Next tram to arrive in forty-five seconds,* the blue light flashes. I hear the hum first and then I spot the tram approaching; sleek and fast, silver with sky blue trim and sparkling windows. The tram pulls up, the doors slide open, I wave good-bye to my dad guy and find a seat on a blue leather cushion. The tram is full of people, all in colorful uniforms with cloud patches embroidered with their names. Some are speaking English, some Spanish, some French.

"Next stop, Skyline," the recorded voice announces. "Restricted area, authorized visitors only." The voice launches into translations as the tram pulls to a stop in front of a platform with the name Skyline in sky blue on a big station sign.

No passengers get out. Just me.

I take the stairs leading up to a platform with an elevator. According to the sign, the elevator requires my fingerprint to open. They couldn't possibly have my fingerprint, but when I press my index finger against the pad, the doors slide open.

Weird.

The inside of the elevator is painted like a mural of blue sky, clouds, and birds in flight. The elevator zips upward so quickly it makes my stomach drop. When the doors open to Skyline, I see how high we are. Through the glass windows are real clouds and the tiny city of Falling Bird below.

The room takes up an entire floor. It's shaped like a cylinder with windows all around and an observation deck. Even the rug is a strange combination of old-fashioned tapestry patterns set into different size circles. There are desks in a ring around the room, with binders and books and computer screens on them. And then out from there are chairs all facing the windows and a vast system of old-fashioned radio switchboards. People with headphones are sitting at some of the radios.

In the very center of the lounge is a huge circular desk where a large man sits. He's got bulky shoulders, dark skin, and a buzz cut, and he's wearing an ordinary plaid shirt. He jumps up when he sees me as if I'm the person he's been waiting for.

"Finn." He pushes a button that opens a door in his round desk for him to walk through. He extends his big hand to me. "I'm Sparky."

He has a friendly handshake and welcoming eyes. I like him immediately.

"You're a guy after my own heart," Sparky says. "I can't tell you how rare it is for someone to exchange dreams for information."

I'm not sure what's so special about this, but I'm glad he likes me. "Yes, sir," I say.

"The thinking, the planning, the organizing . . . all quite commendable."

"And the worrying. Don't forget that." I crack a smile.

"You can call it worry or you can call it foresight. Either way there aren't a lot of twelve-year-old boys who have that skill set. We could really use a sharp young mind like yours around here."

I shrug. I'm not sure what to say. People don't usually appreciate this about me. "How do you know so much about my life?" I ask.

"Computer access, manuals, word of mouth." He points to the stations. "Can't always keep up with the technology you all have, but we're good at capturing information."

"I don't understand how you could have my fingerprint."

"Oh, that's standard stuff. When you push a button in your dream home, your fingerprint is automatically sent to us electronically. The most exciting part of our technology is"—he lowers his voice—"it incorporates the desire component."

"What does that mean?"

"It means it's partially powered by what the user wants." He touches his chest. "In here. Some people call it the heart factor."

I'm trying to figure out how this could even be possible, when Sparky enters my name on a keyboard.

"Let me show you a few things," he says.

A picture of my old house pops up on the big screen facing us. Alongside it, my school, my family, and all of my school photos appear.

"The one question I have is why you didn't go into managing the basketball team. The games never seemed to work for you."

"I like to play."

"Ah yes, dreaming is intoxicating, isn't it? I suppose you want to go home too."

"Of course."

"Let me frame the question differently for you. Is Uncle Red's home?"

I don't want to talk about this, but he's waiting for an answer. "I dunno," I mumble.

"Well look, let's not waste time here. You're off the clock right now, but that will change soon enough. Here's what you need to know. You can come work for me. It's not Headquarters or anything, but it's pretty nice up here.

"Or you can attempt the trip to Uncle Red's. You won't be given the same amount of time as Mouse and India because of the deal you made, so I'd lay odds for you at . . . well, let me first ask, there wasn't a cat in your dream house, was there?"

"What difference would that make?"

"Unpredictable element. Skews the statistics."

"No cat."

"I didn't think so. Let me look at you." He walks in a circle around me, inspecting from every angle. "One in one hundred thousand, given your general physical condition."

"One in one hundred thousand to get to Uncle Red's?" Sparky nods. "Afraid so."

"What are the odds of getting back there?" I point to my old house on the screen.

He shakes his head. "No chance at all. On the other hand, *this*"—he points at the surrounding room—"is a sure thing. One hundred out of one hundred.

"The journey to Uncle Red's will be very, very difficult. Actually, *difficult* doesn't even begin to describe what will be required of you. I wish they could make it easier. People think Headquarters should be able to." He shrugs. "But they can't change the laws of nature any more than I can. I'll do my best, Finn, but if you decide to continue on, there's not much help I can provide."

"I don't understand."

He nods. "Too much information. It's the story of my life. Look, just keep this in mind. If you want to take me up on my offer, pick up a white courtesy phone. If the heart factor is in line, the phone will connect automatically to me. But this isn't a default option. You'll have to choose while you're still on the clock. The people on default—" He shakes his head, his lips pursed. "Their hearts aren't in it."

I look around for a wall clock, a computer clock, a clock anywhere. "What clock?" I ask.

"The puzzle pieces Chuck gave you . . . When you put them together, Chuck will bring you your clock. The clock will let you know how much time you have to make your decision."

"About whether to come here or not?"

"Exactly. If you decide you want to travel to Uncle Red's, you'll need to find the black box within the allotted time."

"What black box?"

"The black box is a simple information receptacle. It will tell you precisely what you need to know. The tricky part is locating it. If you're lucky, you'll get a tunnel dog to help you. Unfortunately, that whole area is out of my jurisdiction. You'll have to deal with Francine on that, I'm sorry to say. And she's not a believer in free will.

"Now, I apologize in advance for the downward motion phase. If you were to decide to opt out right now and come work for me, I could keep you from it." He pauses hopefully.

I look around at this huge observation room. It is tempting. There's something about the order here that appeals to me. I would be a step ahead of everything. I could get control in a way that's simply not possible in ordinary life.

"What about my mom? And Mouse and India?" I try to imagine them up here. Mouse would like it, but I don't think my mom and India would.

Sparky shakes his neatly-clipped head. "You can only make this decision for yourself, Finn."

"I'd never see them again?"

"Too many factors are out of our control to safely determine that."

"No, then?"

"I can't say, Finn. I can gather information, but I don't have a crystal ball."

I nod.

"So what is your decision, Finn Tompkins?"

"I want to stay with my family."

He sighs and puckers his lip up like a little kid. "I

was afraid you'd say that. I hate to have to do this to you, buddy," he mutters.

"Do what?" I ask.

"There's no other way." He squints at me, hesitates for a moment, and then pushes the down key on the keyboard.

A second later I hear a popping sound, like metal rivets being driven somewhere below me. And suddenly the circle of carpet I'm standing on gives way and I'm sucked down into darkness, the wind roaring in my ears.

FINN

CHAPTER 14
THE HEART FACTOR

When I open my eyes, everything aches. Nothing like being dropped from the top of the building, then run over a few times. That's not what happened, but it's what it felt like. My body was traveling so fast in that dark chute that when I slammed down onto the road, it hurt like you can't believe.

I liked Sparky too. Why did he have to push that stupid button? I sure wouldn't want to do that to anyone.

I'm on a narrow street now—an alley full of shops, one jammed against the next. Each shop has a table in front full of dusty signs taped to the tablecloths and propped up around the table skirts. There don't seem to be any customers, just shopkeepers and birds. Buzzards, blue jays, crows, canaries, even a parrot white as coconut cake—the birds are everywhere.

I don't know what the shops are selling. I can't read the signs through my thumping headache. It feels like the loudest music in the world is playing in my head, but I can only feel the vibration it makes. I can't hear the sound.

Just moving triggers little waves in my eyes. But after a few minutes of sitting perfectly still, my vision clears and I focus on the signs. *Relive Your Moment. Return to the Home of Your Dreams. Photos, memories, videos, mementos of your day. Relive Your Day. Return to Euphoria.*

Trying to figure out what they're talking about has distracted me from the pain. I'm just wondering if I can stand up, when I see Mouse. She's piled in a heap at the bottom of another tube a half block away.

"Mouse!" I'm all the way up now, standing in one sudden motion. My vision has gone wobbly again and I feel sick to my stomach. Sharp stabbing pains shoot through my head behind my eyes.

I get to the curb and it all comes up. The apple pie, the French fries, the Philly cheese steak sandwich—all of it in a lumpy, gumpy mess.

"Finn!" Mouse calls. "Are you okay?"

I wipe my mouth on my sleeve and start forward again, my eyes trained on my little sister's wild red hair. Throwing up has made me feel better and so has seeing Mouse. In a burst of adrenaline, I make it down the alley to her.

"Are you okay, Mouse?" I ask.

"My arm hurts. Bing says it's broken."

"Uh-oh, we need to get help."

"You found out how to get home, didn't you, Finn, didn't you? I want to go home to our real house."

I'm not sure she totally understood we were leaving our old home for good, but now doesn't seem like the time to explain it to her.

"First, we have to find India," Mouse rattles on.

"You haven't seen her?"

She shakes her head. "Then we need to put the wood pieces together, like Mr. Chuck said," Mouse fills in.

"That's right, then Chuck comes and he gives us our clocks and we have to find a dog and a black box in a certain amount of time," I tell her.

"Like a game?" Mouse asks.

"Like a game . . . a really important game," I say. "I'm going to go talk to those other shopkeepers down the road. One of them might be able to help."

Mouse shakes her head. "Skye said not to."

"Skye? Who's Skye."

"She's a girl. She was here before. She said don't trust them. She told Bing she heard people talking about India. They want her." Mouse's voice is wistful, one arm tucked against her shirt, like a hurt wing. "You know how pretty she is."

"They want her?" I repeat. "What for?"

"Skye didn't know. She had to leave fast because she saw the cat and she was trying to catch it."

"What cat? This was a visible person? Not one of Bing's friends, right?"

Mouse nods.

Still I wonder. It sounds pretty weird to me. "We've got to get you to a doctor, Mouse," I say firmly. "No matter what this Skye person says.

"We need help!" I call, half running across the street, waving my arms.

One tall shopkeeper switches his open sign to closed and goes in his store. Another shrugs at me and continues sweeping. The rest ignore me. Only the black birds look up.

"One thousand dollars for a second chance," a man with a bushy beard calls hopefully.

"We need a doctor, please!" I tell him. "Or a cell phone." Maybe it's only India's cell that doesn't work. It could need to be charged or else my mom didn't pay the bill.

Or maybe there's a white courtesy phone. Sparky will know what to do!

I scout around until I spot a white phone tucked into a kiosk and I head for it. But when I pick up the receiver, all I get is a fast busy signal.

"Sparky?"

The line doesn't connect. The fast beeps continue. Wait a minute. Sparky said something about the heart factor. I don't want to accept his offer . . . could the phone know that?

I scoot back to Mouse. "Does it hurt a lot?" I ask.

"Only if I move it," she says as I notice a woman with fuzzy black hair and a big hook nose go into her store and come out with a round metal bin.

The woman is heading toward us, the bin in her hand. I hurry to meet her. When I get close I see there are cell phones inside, maybe twenty in all.

She smiles at me, then launches into a long explanation in a foreign language—Russian, I think. The only words I recognize are my own name: Finn Tompkins. She gestures to the cell phones like I should take them.

"Thank you," I say with a sudden, aching gratitude, searching my pockets for something to give her in return. All I have is my Rubik's Cube and my house key—which isn't any good to anyone except maybe the guy who took our house. I hand her the puzzle cube.

She stares at it with fascination. Then I see her digging in her pocket. She pulls out a big stack of laminated cards and riffles through them until she finds the one she wants.

She sees me watching her and hands me the card.

Century Awareness Training—Games, the card says in English and in Russian. It has pictures of dozens of games with instructions and tips for how to win.

Sure enough, the Rubik's Cube is on there. I hand it back to her to read as I fish out a cell phone like my mom's and push the on button. The display doesn't light up. I push down longer and wait. Nothing happens. No beep. No lights. No digital display.

Dead as a can of tomato soup.

I grab another . . . it doesn't respond either. And another and another. I look up at the woman, who is happily turning the yellow and red squares of my Rubik's Cube.

If only I could call my mom. If only she could come.

I'm down to the bottom of the bin. There are only two cells left.

Hey, wait a minute. The heart factor. I really want to talk to my mom. Shouldn't one of these work? I take a deep breath and try the second to last cell. I hold down the on button and it sputters to life. My hand shakes as I dial Mom's number. "Please, please let her answer."

The sound of connecting circuits is the most beautiful sound in the world. The digital display window flashes my mom's cell number. The phone is calling Mom!

But when I blink the numbers rearrange. The new phone number is unfamiliar.

"Enter your name," a mechanized voice commands.

I push the letters that spell Finn Tompkins and wait. The phone beeps again and the computerized voice informs me, "You are not an authorized user."

The line is dead. The phone turns off. It will not turn on again no matter how many times I try.

I pick up the last phone, then look around for a tree like the McFaddens'. There is one that is sort of similar. I stand under it and push the on button, but this cell is dead too.

Mouse is across the way, watching me, trying to

understand what's going on. Where the heck is India? Wasn't she supposed to be here?

What did that girl Skye mean when she said they *wanted* her? Was India offered a position too? Did she take it?

The Russian woman is still engrossed in my Rubik's Cube, oblivious to what I've been doing.

"Hey," I tell her, "I need help."

She seems to understand the tone of my voice. She nods, her dark eyes thoughtful, her face genuinely sorry. She points to the phones hopefully.

I shake my head no. Everyone understands *no*, right?

She nods and gathers them back into her bin. They *clank* as they hit the bottom. She hands my Rubik's Cube back, with one side complete.

"What about you?" I call to the other shopkeepers. "We need help . . ."

But they avert their eyes and return to sweeping the stoops, washing the windows, lettering new signs. The black birds are perched on their shoulders, blue jays scavenging near their feet and finches flying in a cloud around them.

When I get back to Mouse, she's shaking her head in a tiny, firm no. "We've been here longer than you have, Bing and me. We've been watching. Skye is right. We don't trust them either."

Mouse has a point. There's something too eager about them, too hungry. The only one who is nice is the Russian lady.

106

"Finn?" Mouse asks. "What are they selling? Bing can't figure it out either."

"I think they want to sell us another day like we just had."

"How can you sell a day?"

"They sell the chance to be in that fancy house again."

Mouse nods. "How come we only got to stay there one night?"

"Just the way it works here, I guess. Mouse, can you walk?"

She's usually full of energy, jumping and hopping instead of walking. It's strange to see her move so carefully. She seems to be okay, except for that arm, which is hanging a weird way, making me think Bing is right, it *is* broken. I heard an EMT speak at school one time. He said something about making a sling.

I don't have anything to make a sling out of except my hoodie. I take it off, and tie the long sleeves around Mouse's neck so she can rest her arm if she needs to.

She moves forward on stiff legs. "I have to walk without bumps," she reports.

"All right then," I tell her.

Just behind me I see a cluster of vultures like black hunchbacks hopping toward us. "Git!" I holler, and they scuttle back to their perch on the rooftop.

I see in Mouse's eyes that she understands why the vultures are here.

"Bing says to forget about them," Mouse tells me, grabbing my hand with the hand of her good arm.

"That Bing," I say. "He's all right."

CHAPTER 15
BIRDS

That wild tunnel ride was bad. Seriously, I could have been hurt!

I figured it was an earthquake. They're worse near the epicenter, which must have been under the house, because things in that shopping district place didn't seem damaged.

I'm glad Mouse isn't here, because she'd be driving me nuts, asking a billion questions. Everything has to make scientific sense to her, then she spends half her life talking to a friend who doesn't exist. Go figure.

Mouse and Finn were supposed to meet me. They have these white phones around and this announcement came on the loudspeaker. "India Tompkins, please pick up the white courtesy phone." I picked it up and this like recorded voice said: "You are early. Please wait one hour and fifty-six minutes at your current location to connect with the following persons: Finn Tompkins. Mouse Tompkins."

Two hours! Who's going to wait around for two hours?

First thing I did was I met this guy, Mickey, with the black bird that reminded me of that old song my mom plays on the guitar. *Blackbird singing in the dead of night. Take these broken wings and learn to fly.* As soon as I saw those black birds I knew he was okay. The other shopkeepers wanted me to come to their shops too, but I liked Mickey. He had nice eyes and he gave me a good deal.

I would have stayed talking to him longer, only I needed to get back to my cool house so I could check with Maddy. Today is probably Ariana's party. Maddy will freak if I'm not there.

What I don't get is, why is this happening? I don't mean science why. But why why. It's so random. My mom always says you don't just end up someplace like it's magic. You make decisions that got you there.

But Mom is wrong about this. This just happened. I swear.

I asked Mickey about the earthquake, but he said he didn't feel it. He said he had a dream house once and an earthquake hit then too. Isn't that crazy? Then he explained I need to buy a ticket. It costs fifty dollars, which I just happen to have . . . Isn't that cool the way that worked?

The sign said it cost one thousand dollars for one day! But he let me have it for fifty.

Things are a little different in the streets now. None of the movie screens have us on them anymore. They have other people being welcomed to Falling Bird. Who cares about strangers' lives and their trophies for lacrosse and stuff? Oh well, I'll be back in my new home soon. I just wish I could find it.

Mickey gave me a map. I had to walk down the road where all the shops were, up a big hill and down the street with the big homes. The thing is the houses look way different. I think this is mine—it says 401—but my initial isn't on the rock path anymore. The door is painted pale pink instead of lime green. The flowers in the yard are these big white flowers. Mine were small and purple. I totally loved the smell of them too.

Wait, though, I see my cool mom in the window. She looks different. Her hair is up in a French twist. I wonder if she has a new stylist. I wave to her, but she doesn't see me.

The door has no knob, no knocker, and no bell, as if everybody who is supposed to be inside is already. Maybe that part isn't different. The door was open when I came in before, so I didn't notice.

I knock. No one answers.

Finn's and Mouse's places are different too. At home it takes a year to remodel, but here it takes what . . . an hour? I bang on the window, my bracelet clinking against the glass.

Still nothing.

Then I hear a motor hum behind me. When I turn, an electric cart with sky blue upholstery is gunning toward me. The driver steers the cart up on the lawn and squeaks to a halt. He is wearing a midnight blue uniform with a patch of sky blue and a puffy white cloud with his name, Dean, embroidered on it. He has bright, almost neon, blue plastic gloves and an officer's cap. He's big and burly like he spends a lot of time with barbells, but his skin is smooth and young and he has kind eyes—two slivers of green in his square face.

"What are you doing, miss?" he asks.

I tell him about the earthquake and how I fell out of my house. I dig out my ticket and hand it to him. I am totally in the right here.

He sighs. "I'm sorry, young lady," he says, taking my ticket and tearing it in two. "It's worthless. Soon as we crack down on them, they find a new loophole. You wouldn't think they'd have much motivation to steal here." He shakes his head. "No matter where you are, there are crooks, I guess. One or two at every level.

"You know what they use the extra bucks for? Birds. Why they want more birds, I don't know. Cats I could understand. Birds, I'm at a loss. Bird strikes is my best guess. Just jealousy. That's what that's all about."

"Jealousy?"

"People want what they can't have. They make decisions they can't live with. I've been sending in Form fifteen-thirty about them all year, but nobody's done anything about it yet."

"Um, excuse me." I pick up the ticket pieces. "This isn't stolen. I paid for this. See what it says here. *Will admit one to your dream home.*"

"Yeah, I see." He nods, flipping the ticket piece over. "And look here, did you read the fine print? *Void where prohibited.*"

"So?" I shrug. "It always says that." But wait . . . *fine print*. I don't like the sound of this phrase. Isn't that what Mom said got her in trouble with our house?

He crosses his muscular arms. "And where do you think it's prohibited, miss? Take a wild guess."

"I dunno," I mutter, though my stomach doesn't feel so great.

"Here." He taps his metal-toed boot on the grass and shakes his head sympathetically. "Sleazebags."

Wait. This can't be true. I couldn't have wasted our last fifty dollars. What will I tell Finn and Mouse?

"I can get my money back, though, right?" I croak.

"Don't bother," he advises. "Isn't worth messing with scum."

"Oh yes it is!" I shake my finger at him. "I'm getting every dime back. You watch."

"Nobody messes with India Tompkins." He winks at me. "All right then. Hop in and I'll take you where you want to go, Miss India."

I angle my head toward the house. "Can't I go inside first?"

He sucks air into his mouth, seals his lips, and shakes his head. "I'm afraid not."

I give him a flirty smile. "You sure?"

He cocks his head and smiles back. "Yeah, as a matter of fact, I am."

Dean is nice. If I didn't need to get my money back, I'd totally keep talking to him, maybe ask him more about this place, but I have to get down to business here. "We should go then."

He smiles warmly, as if I've completely won him over. "You're a feisty one, missy."

I follow him to his golf cart and climb in on the passenger side. He puts the cart in gear and maneuvers it skillfully down the wide street. It feels good to sit down. I lean back on the cushion and enjoy being driven. I didn't realize how tired I was.

The cart is way fun, but the ride is too short. We're already back at the familiar alley crowded with shops. Dean pulls the cart to a graceful halt and waits for me to get out.

He salutes as if he's in the military. "Give 'em heck, India," he says as he backs his vehicle around.

I smile and wave as he takes off, and then suddenly it hits me. "Hey! Wait! You can't just leave me here!

"Wait! Wait!" I shout, my legs spinning under me, I'm running so fast. I'm gaining on the cart too, but it's impossible to keep up this pace. Dean doesn't turn around. He can't hear me. "Wait! Stop! Dean? Dean person?"

My chest aches. I have to slow down and when I do, the cart zips out of sight.

Something inside me begins to crumble. And then suddenly birds are everywhere. A mass of feathers, beady eyes, and sharp claws.

Beaks clip my ear, my shoulder, the back of my head. Birds peck my arms. Birds dive for my eyes. Big black birds, sharp-eyed blue jays, and vicious brown hawks surround me.

"Bird strike!" somebody yells.

INDIA

CHAPTER 16
PLUM-COLORED PANTS

The birds are gone. I think it was that white cat that scared them away. I take my hands from my face, wondering where the cat is now. I don't see her.

The look on the hawks' eyes as they dove for me was mean. I have pecks on my arms, little torn pieces of skin, and one hawk ripped a hunk of my hair. My wrist is bleeding. I mean seriously, those birds wanted to kill me.

What did *I* do wrong? This is so completely unfair. I need to find Mouse and Finn. We need to get out of here. Weren't they supposed to meet me? It's just like Mouse to wander off. She probably saw some sign she wanted to read.

All I see is a pile of feathers and popcorn on the narrow alley. There aren't a lot of people, unless you count the shop owners. A man wearing the midnight blue uniform is maneuvering a trash can on wheels over to the feathers and popcorn. He sweeps it all into neat piles.

The popcorn reminds me of Maddy. She loves popcorn. She probably insisted Ariana have it at her party. Ariana's party must be over now. They had it without me.

I wave to the guy. "Hello, um, sir!"

"*Bonjour,*" he says.

Oh great, he's French. How do I say I need help in French? I'm supposed to know this. "*J'ai assist,*" I say.

He hands me a broom.

Terrific . . . I just asked him if I could help him.

Then I spot Mickey walking toward me. "India." His face is full of concern. "What happened?"

He's a scummy guy. He probably caused the bird strike. That's what Dean said. I trust Dean, right?

"India," Mickey calls again in his singsong voice with his black greasy hair, his yellow teeth, his motorcycle black eyes, and his pointy beard. I glance over at him—his eyes are mesmerizing. I can't look away.

"I have something to tell you," Mickey reports, beckoning in slow mo. "It's urgent."

I get right in his face and shout. "I want my money back! And call your stupid birds off."

"What are you talking about? What birds?"

"The birds that attacked me."

"Our birds aren't vicious. Who told you that?" he asks.

"Somebody I trust," I say. "I want my money back."

"Oh no!" His mouth freezes in a perfect O. "You didn't let them mislead you. You still have your ticket?"

"Void—void where prohibited. That's what the fine print said. You lied!" An alarm goes off inside my head telling me not to get into this with him, but I can't help myself. People shouldn't get away with cheating you. How dare he!

"Oh." He shakes his head and his eyes well up with tears. "You didn't believe him, did you? Not my beautiful India." The beady eyes of the crow perched on his shoulder are fixated on me.

Why didn't I see what a grease ball he is? I know why . . . it's because of his eyes. They are large, deep, singer-songwriter eyes.

Mickey shakes his head, clucking sadly. "They always try that. They don't want you to have a second chance."

"Second chance," chirps the white parrot perched on a nearby rooftop.

"But why not?" I blurt out before I can stop myself.

"They've got their policies and procedures and they don't like when a person"— his pointer fingers move all around, like fingers gone haywire—"messes with the system, but you know the truth, India."

I hate that this makes sense.

He leans forward hopefully. "You still have your ticket?"

I shake my head.

"No? It's gone. Ohhhhhh . . ." He lets the sound trail off. "Okay, okay. Let me think about this. Maybe old

Mickey can help." He taps his temple then winks at me. "Old Mickey has a trick or two up his sleeve. It has worked before."

If he helps me, I won't have to tell Finn and Mouse I got gypped out of our fifty dollars. If they find that out, they'll tell my mom. She'll have more proof of how stupid I am.

"Maybe I could give you a duplicate." He dangles a new ticket in front of me, smiling. "This is deed to ownership. For just half price."

More money? That's what he wants? Isn't that what the guy on the phone told my mom? The one who said he could make sure they didn't foreclose on our house? Throwing good money after bad, my mom said, but she did it anyway.

I back up, slamming into a white board advertising the special deals.

His big eyes goad me. "India, my India, you shouldn't let them win, no?"

"You're a slime ball!" I shout.

"Ahh well." He wags his head right and left, eyeing my bracelet—the sapphire one my mom gave me for my thirteenth birthday. "Perhaps you want to know what became of your brother and sister."

"Tell me!" I shout. *"You tell me."*

His lips slide in, he nods his head as if he's having a conversation with himself. "You give me the bracelet." He wiggles his finger at me. "And I'll let you know, Miss Beautiful India."

Dean was right. Mickey is a slime bucket. But what else am I going to do? I have to find out where Mouse and Finn are. It's just a stupid piece of jewelry, anyway. I undo the clasp and hand it to him. His fingers close slowly around the sapphire.

He smiles at me, gently, warmly—his smile is powerful. It feels like he's stroking my hair with it. For a second I lose myself in it.

When I blink, he's slipped inside his store. He's locking his locks. *Tchuk, tchuk, tchuk.* "Haven't seen them," he calls through the glass.

I bang on the door so hard the glass trembles. I kick the wood and throw my shoulder against it.

He's inside, laughing at me.

All of the shopkeepers are huddled in their shops. Signs advertising the mementos of your day, and the chance at another, blow in the breeze. The street is deserted except for a handful of small birds searching the ground for birdseed.

Mickey must have seen Finn and Mouse, otherwise how could he know I have a brother and sister? But then, our pictures were everywhere. Maybe he only saw them on the screens.

I look up at the movie playing. A new girl with braces and pigtails is tying her ballet slippers. *Welcome, Rachel*, it says.

I need to talk to Maddy. She totally helps me think through things. She is the best best friend I've ever had.

Wait . . . what did that Chuck dude say? Something

about putting together . . . what was it? Oh, I know. He gave me that hunk of wood, so when I find Mouse and Finn we can assemble the puzzle and he'll come get us.

I feel in my pocket for the wood piece. I need to have it in my hand.

But it's not in my pocket. These aren't my pockets. They aren't my jeans. They're the plum-colored pants like the ones Maddy always wears.

CHAPTER 17
THE EMPTY SCREEN

I don't know when I decide to climb back up the tunnel, but once the idea occurs to me, it seems so simple. Just go back the way I came. They can't have security guys patrolling the tunnel. It's too small. No one else could fit.

When I get back to my house, then I can talk to Mouse and Finn through one of those screens in that downstairs room. We missed each other, but we can arrange a meeting place. I've got this covered. No big deal.

Then I can get my own clothes back. And when we all meet up, I'll have the missing piece. All I have to do is climb up that tunnel, right?

At first it was a little confusing knowing which one was mine. I remember generally where I came out, but not exactly. But then I noticed the address was stamped on the inside: 401.

The tunnel is about ten feet in diameter. At this end, it's parallel with the ground, but soon it begins the steep climb to my house. The sides are shimmery black fabric reinforced with springy coils of wire. It's like a giant Slinky covered in jet-black fabric.

It takes me a little time to get the hang of walking up the cylinder, but eventually I find a way of climbing by pinching the coils with my fingers and digging my toes into the fabric sides. It feels a little like scaling the playground slides, which I used to do when I was little.

The dark is disorienting, but when I'm totally confused, I feel an acorn drop, which gets me back on track. Where did it come from, I wonder. It was almost as if somebody was watching me and knew I needed help.

As I pull myself up, I imagine telling Maddy about this. Pretending to talk to her helps me forget how much my arms ache. I take little breaks. But even resting makes my arms tired, so I keep going.

At last I see a dull flicker of light above, like a flashlight that needs a new battery. I speed up, full of hope, ignoring the nasty voice in my head that tells me Mickey and the other sleazes will be in my dream house now too. Mickey has everything I own that's worth anything, but I won't let him get my house. No way. The light glows brighter as I inch upward coil by coil, my arms shaking. My muscles are so tired but I'm doing this. I'm going to climb right back into my house!

"Way to go, India. Way to go, girl," I tell myself as I pull my legs out of the tunnel into the bedroom suite. The tunnel comes out under my bed, but the bed isn't broken or cracked the way it was when I fell out of it. I guess they repaired it already because it's all in one piece now. Though when I look closely I see a fault line—an uneven crack in the mattress. Must be the repair job. I mean, how do you fix a bed split in two.

This makes me think about the street vendors selling a second chance. It's as if there's a whole industry built around the loss of your home. How disturbing is that?

I have to scoot on my belly to get out into my room, which looks totally different now. The bed is in the same place. The chair, the window seat, and the bathroom are too, but the decor is different. There's a white satin comforter with pink bows, flouncy pillows, white lacey curtains, and a white shag rug. Ballerinas and pink ribbons are everywhere. Nothing about the room says me.

Then I see the cat, her white fur an exact match to the rug. Is this the same cat that scared off the birds? If so, how did she get back up here? The cat's tail flicks, and something jingles around her neck. Her green eyes watch me as if she knows something I don't. Next to her is a package wrapped in lime green paper, tied with bright pink and orange polka-dot ribbon and marked with the wild lettering they use for me.

India, the tag reads.

I tear it open. Inside are my jeans with my cell phone and the puzzle piece safely in the pocket. And there's something else too. A tiny computer screen with a wristband—a cross between a watch and a computer.

I buckle it on my wrist and as soon as I tuck the end of the strap in, up pops Maddy, her corkscrew curls bouncing around her face.

My knees collapse under me. "Maddy, oh Maddy. This is so awful you can't believe it," I blubber from where I sit like a lump on the carpet.

"In? What's going on?" she asks.

"I'm moving to Colorado," I sob.

"Look, this is a terrible connection. I thought you said you were moving to Colorado. Tell me where you are. I need to come over right now," Maddy says.

She can totally hear how upset I am.

"But Maddy . . . I'm at four-oh-one, that's all I know . . . it's like this big street. Four-oh-one some road."

"Find the street name, In. My mom will take me," she says, but the screen image is fading until I can hardly see her.

"Maddy! Maddy!" I call, but she's gone. There's only me yelling at an empty gray square on my wrist.

The cat is busy licking her paws. Her eyes glow green. Around her neck I notice the ring my cool mom was wearing, tied with a ribbon. She gets up and stretches, her tail in the air, as if she has all the time in the world.

I try to grab her, but she leaps easily out of my reach.

"Finn and Mouse," I whisper to the little screen, but nothing happens. There are no buttons or dials. It isn't a touch screen. I try to flip up the side or slide open the bottom, but this device is as smooth as an eyeball.

"Maddy," I whisper again and again. But the screen stays dark.

"Finn and Mouse," I enunciate as clearly as I can. I even write Mouse's and Finn's names in the air above it.

Downstairs in that room with all the screens, I never had to do anything. The right faces were just there.

That's where I need to go.

But this is somebody else's house now. The screens probably have that person's friends.

I tiptoe to the door of the bedroom, and look out past the giant hall to the staircase.

The cat watches me as if she's wondering what I'll do. I take a deep breath and scoot out of the room, but the second my toe hits the first step, an alarm rings. It's loud—a series of repetitive bips with answering beeps like an alarm and its mating call. I pull my toe back, run through the bedroom to the bathroom, and lock the door. The lock breaks off in my hand, which totally freaks me out because now I hear somebody's coming.

I huddle in the corner of the bathroom and listen to the approaching footsteps and commanding voices.

The shadows shift in the sliver of light under the door. And then all at once the door shoots open, banging against the wall. Men in midnight blue uniforms with white cloud patches and blue gloved hands stand outside.

"India Tompkins, you are in violation of code number seven-five-two-two," they say. "You need to come with us."

MOUSE

CHAPTER 18
THE MARVINS

One of the Marvins has India. There were six Marvins on the screen. All Boy Marvins, but I've seen Girl Marvins here too.

India is going to be mad. If that many policemen have you in custardy, that will definitely go on your record and you won't be able to get your driver's license.

I wish my arm didn't hurt. I wish every time I wanted to cry, Bing didn't tell me *Don't be a crybaby*.

I tell Finn that we need to get in trouble so the Marvins will come and take us to India. Finn says that's not a good idea. He says it will be easier to get her out if we aren't locked up too.

Did they take India to jail? When I saw her on the

big TV her hair needed brushing. Maybe they took her to the hair salon?

We have been walking a long time. When I ask Finn *Do you know where we're going?* he walks faster and pretends not to look at the street signs.

Now Finn is asking a Marvin about India. "What did he say?" I ask when Finn comes back.

Finn pushes his hair out of his eyes. "Shhh, Mouse, I need to think."

"I can help, you know." I raise my good arm. "I am good at thinking. I have a muscle for it right here." I point to my brain.

He nods the way Mommy does when she is driving someplace she has never been before.

I take his hand and hold it tight. I am not a scaredy cat, but I would pretty please like to go home now. "When are we getting India back?" Bing wants to know. He's not going any further until we have a plan. Bing likes a plan.

A new person flashes on the movie screen, but for a half a second in between I see India looking at a tiny screen buckled to her wrist.

"Did you see that?" I ask.

"What?"

"India on the screen." When Finn looks up, she's gone. There's only the girl snowboarding.

"What was she doing?" Finn asks.

"Looking at her wrist, which had a funny watch on it," I answer.

"She doesn't wear a watch," Finn says.

"I know," I say. "But she had one up there." I point at the big screen.

He scratches his head.

He doesn't have a plan yet. I am going to have to help. "Finn, can I see the puzzle Mr. Chuck gave you?" I hold out my hand.

Finn wiggles his fingers into his pocket and he pulls out his wooden tree puzzle. It has a tiny green branch just like mine does. They are twins except they don't look alike. We sit on the curb and snap the pieces together. We turn the two-thirds puzzle all around, but we can't tell what it will be until we get India's piece.

Just holding Mr. Chuck's puzzle in my hand, I feel better. Bing feels better too.

CHAPTER 19
A CRANE

Where did they take India? The police station? The security office? The court? And why? What did she do?

Sparky could tell me exactly what's going on. But I'm afraid if I pick up a white courtesy phone he will think that's because I've decided to go work for him. Right now, I feel so discouraged I almost want to. What if the phone knows that?

The white courtesy phones are everywhere, tucked in alcoves, mounted on the sides of buildings, at the tram stations. You don't notice unless you're looking for them. They fit right in with the city.

Almost everyone here is in uniform and a lot of

them are security. I hope they don't decide to cart off Mouse and me. I talked to one security guy already and he didn't arrest us but he didn't tell me anything either.

The uniform colors clearly signify something. Weather seems to be a big theme. All of the brightly colored vests and tunics have embroidered badges that show rain, snow or sun, fog, clouds, lightning, hail, wind, or rainbows.

I ask a tall blond girl with a lavender tunic and a rainbow badge, "Where is everyone going?"

"To the welcoming," she says. "All the welcomings are held at the amphitheater unless there are too many arriving at the same time," she explains helpfully. "Are you looking for someone?"

"My sister India."

"Long dark hair, about my age?" the tall girl asks.

I nod.

"She's a welcomer now. Lucky duck. She'll be wearing a blue tunic." The girl smiles at me as if just having a sister as a welcomer has suddenly made me someone special.

I guess when we arrived, there were other people being welcomed, so they took us directly to our houses. I wonder who else arrived when we did. Falling Bird is a lot bigger than I thought. I could see that when I was in Skyline.

The streets are mobbed today—the crowd is so large not everybody can fit in the amphitheater, so people spill out into the nearby streets. The video screens are full of the face of the new arrival, singing karaoke, taking her first step as a toddler, doing tricks on her skateboard.

It feels like a spirit rally—like I'm attending the basketball playoffs at the high school. Only then I'm excited to be there and now I just want to grab India and get away from all of this.

There is a swarm of security people in carts and on foot, plus the welcomer people in blue tunics, and others in yellow and green and lavender tunics with suns and moons on their badges. Mouse and I walk by a choir of blue-tunic welcomers. They are practicing harmonizing a chanting song for the new arrival. A woman in a yellow-sun tunic cups her hand behind her ear and points to the sopranos to sing louder.

"Jew-elll, Jew-elll, you so ruuu-elll," the choir sings. "Cooo-elll, coo-elll, that's our Jew-elll."

"How are we going to find India?" Mouse asks as we wade through the packed crowd. "What color is she wearing again?"

"Blue," I tell her as we climb up high in the amphitheater, combing the crowd for a beautiful girl with long, brown straight hair.

"Maybe she's not here," Mouse says in a small voice.

"We'll find her. It's like playing I Spy, Mouse, and you're good at I Spy."

"I spy a lot of people who aren't India," Mouse grumbles.

"Look for her hair," I suggest.

"I'm looking for her hair. Bing is looking for her

hair too. Hey wait! There she is! There! There!" she squeals, pointing down to the pit, where a girl with long dark hair and a blue welcomer tunic is unfurling a banner that says: *Welcome, Jewel.* The way she tosses her hair, this is definitely India.

"Why would she want to be a welcomer?" I ask.

"I told you they wanted her," Mouse says. "Everybody wants India."

"Careful of your arm, it's awful crowded down there," I tell Mouse.

"Bing will go first to get people out of the way," she informs me, holding her arm carefully.

It's slow going once we get to the pit, but Mouse is so small she ducks under and through. Even with a broken arm, she's fearless. That's how badly she wants to see India.

India is surrounded by girls in blue tunics. They are all holding hands and laughing. India looks like she fits right in—like these girls are all good friends of hers. How could India make friends so fast?

A man with red blond hair, freckles, and a yellow-sun vest is talking. The name on his sun badge is Laird. "Project that love outward toward the new citizen. Wrap your heart around them. Make them feel—"

"India!" Mouse pushes in between them, holding her arm protectively.

"Oh, hi." India smiles an easy smile, as if she isn't the least bit surprised to see us. "I got a job," she says, her voice radiating excitement.

"Who have we here?" Laird raises his silky eyebrows at India. He takes my hand and pumps it. He tries to shake Mouse's hand, but she won't give it to him.

"This is my brother and—" India tells Laird as the big screens go dark and the first flashing countdown reverberates out of the speakers. When the crowd sees this, they go wild, hooting and hollering and jumping up and down as the numbers flash in neon yellow.

Laird—his hands a-flutter—streaks over to another welcomer, to give her last-minute instructions.

"India!" Mouse is so excited to see India, she seems not to even hear the deafening roar of the crowd. "Give us your twig puzzle, then Mr. Chuck will come and take us home."

"Look." India points to the screen, which shows the skywritten messages for Jewel. "Jewel's coming. I don't want to miss her."

"Jewel? What do you care about Jewel? You've never even met her," I say.

"India! Don't be crazy!" Mouse shouts. "We have to go home!"

"No, wait, look!" India's eyes are charged. *Countdown minute nine* flashes on.

"Nine," the crowd shouts in unison, their voices exploding from their chests.

This is wacko. We finally find India and she's obsessed with a complete stranger. She hasn't even said anything about Mouse's arm.

"India, come on!" I shout.

"No, Finn, listen! Do you know how hard it is to get this job?"

"What job?"

"Welcomer, can't you see?" She fingers her blue tunic. *India*, it says in the same handwritten embroidery all the Falling Bird uniforms have.

"What kind of a job is that?"

"Are you kidding me? It's a great job. Thousands of people wanted it. They were standing in a line two blocks long, but Laird picked me. He loves the way I sing!" Her eyes are open wide, drinking it all in. "And you know what else? They said I could work up to a cool mom position someday. Then I could live in that great house all the time."

"Mouse's arm is broken, India."

"They'll fix it when she becomes a citizen."

"I don't want to be a citizen," Mouse chimes in. "I want to go home!"

My voice shakes. "We're going to Uncle Red's, India."

"Oh yeah, Finn . . ." India snorts, sounding like her real self now. "Do you actually think Uncle Red wants us?"

"Minute seven, Jew-ellll." Laird's fist pumps the air.

"We have to find Mom," I tell her. "Mom wants us. And what about Maddy? You'll never see her again if you stay here."

"Maddy . . . are you kidding? I'm going to invite her. She'll love Falling Bird."

"She's not coming here and you know it."

"Don't you see, Finn? *This* is for sure. What's it going to be like at Uncle Red's? You don't even know. Besides, Uncle Red wanted us to come here. He hired Chuck."

That doesn't make sense, but then none of this makes sense.

India's eyes are back to the screen again, staring at the new girl, Jewel.

"You think that Jewel person is ever going to care about you the way we do?" I ask.

India shrugs but she's already drifting away from us. "There will be another after Jewel. And another after that. Always someone to welcome," she says.

"India." I chase after her through the thick crowd of cheering people. "You can't stay here."

"You can get a job, Finn. Maybe you could be a driver. Even Mouse can drive here. They make cars so even little kids can reach the pedals."

Jewel is on the screen competing in some kind of spelling relay. She's spelling the word *prosciutto*.

"See how smart she is." India points proudly.

"India. I'm smarter than that. I can spell *hors d'oeuvres*," Mouse says. "H-O-R—"

"Don't you see . . . it doesn't matter?" India asks. "It's not your day anymore, Mouse. Look at Jewel! Isn't she adorable? Jewel, it's me, India!" India waves her arms in the air.

The crowd presses in on us. They chant, "Jew-elll!" The chant swells louder and louder. "Jew-elll! Jew-elll! You're so coo-elll!"

But India's attention is on the screen, which is showing a distant feather taxi carrying Jewel to Falling Bird. It cuts back to the skywriting—*Welcome, Jewel*—and then to the highway with the trucks with hearts around Jewel's name.

Mouse's eyes squint as if she's searching for a way out of this.

"India," Mouse shouts over the noise. "Maddy called. She says that Brendan really likes you."

"I just talked to Maddy, Mouse. She's going to try to come," India mumbles, her eyes on Jewel's taxi moving across the screen.

"How? How could you talk to her?" I ask.

In the background, the security guys in carts patrol the perimeters. There are hundreds of them and yet they seem to fade into the background like puzzle-piece edges in a finished puzzle.

My hands find the two green twigs with their leafy tops linked together in my pocket. The connected parts are warm—almost as if there's a heartbeat locked inside. It's comforting to touch them. I pull them out and hand them to India. I don't know what else to do.

Her hands won't take them. You can't make someone grab something they don't want.

Out of the press of people, Laird's red blond head

bobs toward us, his quick blue eyes taking stock of the situation.

"India, I've got your back. You don't have to worry anymore." Laird's voice is honey-coated steel. He breaks into a run, headed for her.

"We need you, India. We can't do this without you," I tell her, dodging in front of Laird, blocking him, protecting her. Mouse wiggles her good hand into India's pocket.

"Get away from me, Mouse!" India pushes her out of the way, sending India's piece of puzzle wood flying through the air.

"Ow!" Mouse screams. "My arm!"

A big man in an orange vest, his eyes glued to the screen, steps back to allow a cart to pass. His thick rubber sole lands on the delicate wood piece, splitting it almost in two.

Laird stops, his face stricken. "India, don't leave. You won't get another chance like this one."

I duck under a woman's arm and race to Mouse. Together she and I try to connect the pieces. It's hard to figure it out with one damaged. We fiddle until the cracked piece clicks with ours.

The wood pieces form a crane with the broken piece hanging down like a limp leg. A top notch of leaves that look like feathers appear when the pieces are joined. The bird is still wooden, still inanimate, but an internal mechanism has connected, launching circuitry that creates the bird's flying motion. The bird's motor hums as we watch the mechanical crane fly away in an awkward off-balance trajectory.

Laird sees the bird. His eyes scan the road. "Well, India, what are you going to do now?" he asks when our feather taxi appears.

Mouse has a fistful of the fringe from India's vest, which is under her welcomer clothing. Out of the corner of my eye, I see Laird's blue eyes. He tracks us as we pile into Chuck's taxi. He's still watching as we drive away.

CHAPTER 20
PASSENGER TIME

Why are we back with this Chuck dude in his pinky cab? That welcomer job was so cool. I even liked the blue tunic! Laird picked me for the job. He thinks I have talent. Maddy was going to come too.

Now all I have is a blinding headache and a wrist screen with a mind of its own. If only I could figure out how to turn it on. I have to think the right thoughts for it to switch on, but what are the right thoughts?

I tilt the screen away from Mouse. I don't want her to see. But I can't get it to turn on, no matter what I do. Ahh! I am so totally frustrated. I just barely keep from tossing the screen out the window.

The Chuck dude glances in the rearview mirror and asks in his chipper voice, "So where to?"

We're pulling out of Falling Bird—out onto the open highway. But my head is still inside the screen. I barely register the question.

"We have to find the black box. Isn't that right, Finn? Isn't it?" Mouse chirps.

"What are you talking about?" I ask.

"Look," said Mouse. "We have the clocks just like you said, Finn. And now we're going to play the game with the black box." Mouse runs her hand over the clock imbedded in the back of the front seat. That's the one new thing about the feather taxi. Each of us has a clock facing us. They're four inches across and they look like old-fashioned pocket watches, except they're digital. The covers have our names engraved in Falling Bird font. But here's the weird part: The clocks aren't keeping time, they're counting down.

"How come Finn has less time?" Mouse asks.

"That's the arrangement he made," Chuck says.

"What arrangement?" I ask.

"You'll have to ask Finn about that, but the clocks tell you when you've become a citizen," Chuck explains.

"What arrangement?" I ask, leaning forward to make eye contact with Finn, who is on the other side of Mouse.

He shrugs. "I traded time for information."

"What are you talking about?"

"What am *I* talking about? Why would you want to be a citizen?" Finn counters.

"It's a privilege," Chuck replies in his chipper voice.

"Exactly," I add.

"So if we're not citizens, what are we?" Finn wants to know.

"Passengers," Chuck says.

"Passengers in the car," Mouse adds.

"That's right," Chuck says. "Most passengers decide to stay in Falling Bird and become citizens."

"Oh, no," Mouse says. "We want to go home. Don't we, Finn? We have to find the dog and the box and go home, right, Finn? Right?" Mouse asks.

"Mouse, just be quiet and let Chuck talk," I say.

"Actually, India, she knows as much about it as I do," Chuck says.

"Oh, that's comforting," I say.

"Why wouldn't you know?" Finn asks as the cab picks up speed. "This is your job . . . you must have done this before."

"You're the first passengers I've had who wanted to go back. Most of them are content to become citizens by now. To be honest, I bent the rules a bit to get this far," Chuck says.

"How'd you bend the rules?" I ask.

Chuck glances in the rearview mirror. His eyes find mine. "The bird didn't fit together quite right, India. One of the pieces was broken."

"But it flew," Mouse offers.

"Yes," Chuck agrees. "But not very well. India's piece was damaged and . . ."

"Wait, India! Listen!" Mouse bonks me with her good arm. "Bing says your cell is ringing. C'mon, India! Quick! Answer it!" she shouts in my ear.

Just to humor her, I wiggle the cell out of my pocket and click it open. For a second it flashes on. *139 missed calls* it says before it dies again.

Mouse is freaking. "Bing says it was Uncle Red calling. Bing says he's trying to get through. Mom and Uncle Red are calling and calling and calling."

Chuck is rubbernecking from the front seat trying to see what's happening.

Mouse squeezes my arm so tightly she's totally cutting the circulation off. "Try again!" she cries.

All of us are huddled over my cell as I click the on button. The thought that my cell could work, that I could actually talk to my mom, makes my skin prickle in a way that feels either irritating or nice, I don't know which.

"Let me try," Finn says, and I pop the cell in his hand, but he can't get it to work either.

Everybody shuts up after that. Even the road is quiet. No cars.

Finn hands my phone back to me. "We need to know . . ." Finn insists, "how to find the black box."

"Oh that, yes. I only know what I've heard. On the slow nights the cabbies talk. Hard to say if it's true . . ." Chuck's voice trails off.

"If what's true?" I ask.

"I don't know that much about it," Chuck says. "I

143

haven't seen it in the book, but I'm only halfway through. CA is hard. Technology changes so fast. They're always sending updated versions—2.0, 3.0, 4.0."

"What are you talking about?" I ask.

"CA. Century Awareness. You got to keep up on technology, word usage, politics, or they don't let you work with the public."

"I don't get it, you're a kid, aren't you?" Finn says. "Why are you worried about keeping up?"

"I've been twelve longer than you have," Chuck explains.

"His birthday must be soon. Yours is in October. That's why he's been twelve longer than you have, Finn, right, Mr. Chuck?" Mouse offers. "But, Mr. Chuck." Mouse taps his shoulder. "What do you know about the black box?"

The Chuckinator shrugs, his attention riveted to the road. "Looks like they're making us stop," he mutters, hitting the brakes.

Up ahead is a fence maybe twenty feet high, made of shiny rounded metal with windows in a neat row. Luggage carts, passenger carts, white pearlescent carts are parked in a cluster. A bunch of guys in security uniforms like Dean's go in and out of the two glass booths in front of the fence. A glass tower looms high above us. There are no other cars out here. It's only our feather taxi pulling up to what looks like a border crossing checkpoint station with an opening like the passenger door on an aircraft.

"Maybe they want to know if we have any grape-fruits," Mouse suggests. "Remember when we drove to Mexico and we had the grapefruit and we had to give it to the border man?"

Chuck brings the taxi to a halt and one of the security dudes sticks his head in Chuck's window. He's a short, middle-aged Hispanic guy with black hair straight as a ruler and a uniform shirt tight across his middle. His cloud patch says his name is Manny. "Destination?" Manny asks.

"Airport, sir," Chuck answers.

Manny stares at me. His eyebrows waggle on his face. "With a full load?"

"Passenger's request, sir," Chuck replies.

"Hey, fourteen," Manny calls back to another guard. "They're set for an airport return. Should we check with Francine?"

"Passengers identified?" a mechanical voice like the one in Maddy's dad's GPS answers. Only this one is loud like it's coming through a speaker system.

"The Tompkins kids," Chuck answers.

"All three of them?" the mechanical voice with its perfectly spaced pauses asks.

"Yes, sir," the Chuckinator replies. He's so polite. Not even Finn is that polite.

"India was given a position as a welcomer," the voice states.

My forehead gets hot when I hear my name. My tongue feels dry as dirt.

145

The Manny guard dude sticks his head in the window again. "A welcomer . . . coveted position, India. Going to toss it away"—he snaps his fingers in my face—"like that?"

The screen on my wrist has gone live with the face of Maddy in Technicolor. "In," she says, "my mom has the car out. Just tell me where to go. You are way more fun than Lizzie. You're my best friend forever." But her face is wavering as if there's electronic interference.

"India?" Manny repeats, a question in his voice.

"Yes, sir," I say.

"You won't get another job like that one, honey." His voice is gentle. "You sure you want to turn in your uniform?"

I think about that job. Nothing was hard. Nothing was expected of me that I couldn't easily master. I couldn't fall short. I just did what Laird said. No one thought I was stupid either. My mom always says: If life gives you lemons, make lemonade. But there were no lemons. No reason to make lemonade. The only thing missing was Maddy. And she's going to come, right?

"India, do you want to reconsider?" The mechanical voice rings in my head. I can't tell if the voice is inside or outside my brain.

"Of course she wouldn't," Mouse answers, worming her hand into mine.

"Maddy," I whisper to the empty screen. "What should I do?"

"She's not coming!" Mouse locks the door.

146

"This isn't something anyone else can decide for you, India," Manny explains. He gently moves Mouse's hand, unlocks the door, and reaches inside to pop my clock out of the backseat. This he places carefully in my lap and waits.

"India." Finn's voice is tight as twisted rope. "You won't be going back to that mansion."

The door is open, the path in front of me is flooded with light. Where did it come from? I didn't notice it until now.

The warmth is intense . . . intoxicating. Nothing hurts. There is no pain. The glowing path smells of chocolate cake just out of the oven. It feels like a warm river flowing inside my skin, like my knees are sinking into a feather pillow, like all my hopes have suddenly come true in one dot of the *i* in my name: *India*.

I wrap my fingers around my clock and open the door. There's nothing else to do.

CHAPTER 21
WEATHER ALERT

Mouse's face is so pale she looks as if she's been dusted in flour. "What about India? We can't leave India."

"Threat level orange for continuing vehicles. Threat level orange," the mechanical voice drones on.

Manny sticks his head back in the window. "Pretty cold out there. Snow flurries, according to the Weather Group. And the explosive potential is ninety to ninety-five percent. The Operations Group has their concerns as well."

Chuck's eyes are full of questions. "Shall I take you back to Falling Bird, Finn Tompkins?"

Just behind us at the border station is a white courtesy phone. My heart thumps so loudly I can't hear anything but my own doubts.

"No." I shake my head.

"Finn!" Mouse spits at me. "We can't leave her."

Chuck turns back to the guard. "If you don't mind, sir, they want to continue on."

"Finn!" Mouse pounds on my chest with her good fist.

"Unwilling passenger alert! Unwilling passenger alert! Would Mouse Tompkins like to return to Falling Bird?" the mechanical voice booms.

Mouse grabs my arm with her good hand so tightly each of her fingers feels like they are carving grooves in my flesh. "No," she says. "I'm staying with Finn."

"India needs a sure thing," I tell Mouse. "We have to get the black box first. Then she'll come."

Mouse's voice is so small I almost can't hear it. "What if we can't find it, Finn? What then?"

The guard looks at his clipboard, then down at Mouse. He squats so he can look into her eyes. "Arm bothering you, little one?" he asks softly.

"Can you help her?" I whisper.

"Course. Got full health coverage for citizens. Everybody's shipshape in Falling Bird."

"But then we have to go back?" I ask.

"I'm afraid so," Manny says.

Mouse is huddled up against the door, a crumpled heap of dirty blue corduroy. "You want me to go back with you, Mouse?" I ask her.

"Which way is Mommy?"

"Mommy's that way," I say, pointing away from Falling Bird.

She nods. "That's what Bing says too."

"You're set to go then, little Mouse?" Manny asks.

"Yes, Mr. Manny, sir," Mouse says.

"And, Chuck, you checked with air traffic control? No flights coming in for you, number forty-four?"

"Not yet, sir." Chuck smiles his usual smile, but his hands on the wheel are trembling.

Manny scratches his chin. His eyes are thoughtful, like my mom's when she really wants to know what I think. "All right then. This is your choice," he says, pushing a button in the glass booth. The gigantic door in the metal fence opens and Chuck drives through.

The wheels had been hovering over the road, but now they connect directly to the highway on the other side and the temperature drops sharply. Chuck cranks up the heat. Flying bugs hit the glass and he turns on the windshield wipers.

What are we doing? One hundred thousand to one, Sparky said. Who in their right mind would take those odds? Maybe India was right.

The bugs crunch against the wipers, and the whistling wind batters the car, almost lifting us sideways. All of Chuck's attention is on the road when the radio comes alive. "Forty-four? Dispatch here. Come in, forty-four. Forty-four!"

"Oh no! Not Francine . . . Finn, get the radio!" Chuck shouts. He needs both hands on the wheel to keep the car on the road. "Tell her to put the call through to Sparky."

Sparky? This won't count, right? This isn't a white courtesy phone.

"Forty-four, this is Francine. The Weather Group has requested an immediate return to Falling Bird," she announces. "The threat level has been modified. We are now at threat level red."

I wiggle out of the seat belt and pull the receiver toward me. The curly cord stretches taut. "Um, ma'am, could we speak to Sparky, please?"

The wind howls. Hailstones the size of jawbreakers hit the windshield. The few bugs left are bludgeoned to death by ice pellets.

Chuck seems to need brute strength just to keep the car on the road.

"Mechanical alert!" Francine's voice is panicked now. She doesn't seem to have heard me. Did I push the right button to transmit?

"Come in, forty-four. Vehicle Performance Group confirms your vehicle is not made to withstand the crushing forces of this storm. Forty-four! Threat level red. Return requested immediately."

Chuck's neck swivels for a quick look at me. "How much time do you have?"

"Eight hours, seventeen minutes for me. Nine hours,

seventeen minutes for Mouse," I tell him over the pounding hail pelting down on the windshield. "If we go back, will there be time to try again after the weather breaks?" I shout.

"Doubtful. It will take time to find the black box!"

"What about India?" Mouse cries. "We can't leave her."

"Human Performance Group has their concerns about your behavior, forty-four." Francine's radio voice buzzes. "Please turn back your vehicle. Return requested immediately. Federal laws prohibit tampering with—"

Chuck grips the wheel with one hand. With the other, he reaches up and switches the radio off.

The defroster struggles to keep the windshield from fogging up. The feathers on the hood ornament are flattened straight back with the force of the gale.

I'm panting, trying as hard as I can not to panic. I hang the radio receiver over the front seat. My heart is hammering. "Where is the black box?"

"Near the airport, I think!" Chuck shouts, but we can barely hear his voice.

"You think?"

Chuck shrugs.

"How do we find it?"

"It emits a sound, like a radio beep." Chuck strains to be heard over the howling wind. "The tunnel dogs can hear it."

I crack the window and the icy air bites through my shirt sleeves. How will a dog hear the beep of the black box over this? A new sound like lawn mowers on full power roars in my ear. And then I see the Black Hawk helicopters gunning for us.

"They're coming down," Chuck hollers. "They'll take us back. Look, you have to decide right now what you want to do."

I grab Chuck's shoulder. "What if you go back? Can *you* get India, while we find the black box?"

"I can't make her come with me, Finn. It's her choice. And you and Mouse won't last out here without the car!"

"Leave the car then!" I shout.

"They'll chase the car. It's Falling Bird property. They won't go after you if you're on foot . . ."

"Mouse, you go back and convince India! I'll find the black box," I tell her as the Black Hawk helicopters hover over our heads like mechanical birds of prey.

"I'm not leaving you!" Mouse cries as the hail turns to snow, which makes the highway slick and the tires slip and slide over the road.

"This is crazy, Mouse. We won't survive. Look at it out there."

"I'M STAYING WITH YOU!" Mouse shouts, her good hand clamped around my arm.

"Find the tunnel dogs. Win them over. They'll lead you to the box, but you're going to need a vehicle . . ."

"Where are the tunnel dogs?"

"In the Bird's Nest Passage. Get the dog first, then worry about the vehicle. That's my best guess."

"Your best guess?" I cry.

"Look, Finn, be careful. Not everyone wants you to make it. Francine . . ." But the chop-chop of the helicopters drown out the rest.

I pop my clock out of the seat. I have to take it with me, just like India took hers. It feels a part of me in some creepy way. Mouse grabs hers too as the helicopters land in a whipping rush. Snow blows through the open window.

Chuck floors the taxi. The tires squeal and skid, then grip the ground as he drives off the road, steering between two landing helicopters, over the muddy, snow-dusted terrain to a clearing in the woods.

The helicopters are powering down, the great engines humming at a lower octave. Now that they've made contact with the ground, they can't power up again quickly enough.

"We'll send Bing back!" Mouse shouts in my ear over the deafening noise.

She digs in her pocket for Bing's wallet.

"Mouse, stay with Chuck. You won't make it out here with your broken arm."

"NO! I'M NOT LEAVING YOU!" she shouts. "Chuck, when you find India, give her Bing's wallet." She presses the wallet into his hand.

Chuck takes the wallet. He opens his door and the wind blasts the freezing rain in. Big smothering blankets of snow are coming down in some places. We don't even have jackets.

"Are you sure, Finn?" Chuck cries.

"Yes!" Mouse and I both shout and Chuck dodges to a tree stump. He shoves it out of the way, revealing the entrance to a tunnel. Mouse takes my hand and together we run through the driving wind to the tunnel opening.

"Good luck," Chuck shouts. His words sift through the storm to us.

The helicopters have landed again, closer now. They surround the clearing. Men in blue gloves are running toward us. "Bing, get India!" Mouse cries.

Chuck nods as the wind lifts off his cap. He waves Bing's wallet and slips it into his jacket pocket. "I'll try!" he calls as he runs back to the feather taxi, the men in blue gloves swarming in on him now.

The last thing we see before we descend into the tunnel is Chuck being led away.

CHAPTER 22
BIRD'S NEST PASSAGE

From outside, the tunnel opening looked like an oversized gopher hole. But inside, there's a wide stairwell that takes us down to an underground passageway. The temperature down here is perfect—warm and cozy after the freezing sleet and battering wind outside, maybe because the walls are made of bits of sticks and feathers and stray fluff like a bird's nest, insulating us from the outside.

We don't see anyone now, but clearly people work here. The place looks like the basement floor of an office building for bird people. Cots with bird egg-patterned sheets, tables constructed from egg cartons, feather-covered coat stands, and chairs made of telephone poles with telephone-wire line backs rest against both sides of the passage. Rain gear hangs neatly in a line up ahead; coats with badges that show lightning striking clouds hang on hooks and boots rest in a row on the floor. There's even a cuckoo clock and egg-shaped lockers painted in colors like robin's egg blue, speckled brown, and eggshell white.

There are no dogs down here. No dog hair. No dog dishes. No dog leashes and no dog smell.

I don't bring this up to Mouse, though. I don't want to worry her. She's already walking too slow. I check my clock. Seven hours and fifty-three minutes to find the dogs, find the box, and find India.

"Do you think they'll hurt Bing?" she asks, sitting down on a chair with faded cloud-patterned fabric on the seat by a display of brightly-colored bird houses.

We're in a weird underground world hoping to get help from a pack of strange dogs. We may never see Mom or India again and Mouse is worried about her imaginary friend? As smart as Mouse is, I don't think she gets how important this all is.

"They won't hurt Bing." That is actually the one thing I'm sure about. How could they hurt him? He's imaginary.

"But, Mouse, we need to keep walking."

She doesn't move.

I stare at the scuffed brown bird's nest pattern on

the linoleum. "Bing will be okay. India will take care of him."

"You don't believe that," she says, her chin jutting out, her shoulders slumping down.

I have to admit she's right, I don't believe it. I try again. "Maybe Bing doesn't have to be gone . . . Why don't you call him back?"

She looks at me incredulously. "He does what he wants, Finn. I can't *make* him do anything."

"Yes, you can, Mouse, you made him up."

She shakes her head emphatically. "I did not. He just came to me. It was *his* idea."

What do I say to that? I push my hair out of my eyes, and try again. "You told him to go with Chuck to find India. That was the right thing to do."

She nods. "Finn?"

"Yes, Mouse."

Her eyes well up with tears. "I miss Mommy and India."

"If you love India that much, why do you bug her all the time?"

"I have to," she says, "or she forgets about me."

"I'm not sure that's the best strategy."

Mouse nods as if she's considering this. "Some things are hard to understand." She sighs a grown-up sigh. "That's Bing's job. He thinks about things that don't make sense. I think about things that do."

"Does Bing have a brother? Maybe his brother can

158

come help you, because really, Mouse, we have to keep moving."

"Bing's a private person. He doesn't talk about his person life."

Just my luck. My sister's imaginary friend is a hermit.

I'm about to try another tack when a bell rings in the distance and the sound of approaching footsteps echos through the passageway.

"Someone's coming," Mouse whispers.

Our eyes skitter around the long twig-covered hallway. The lockers? I try several until I find two that are open.

"Here," I whisper to Mouse. She slips inside and I close the door as quietly as I can behind her. I slide into the locker next to hers. My locker bangs when it closes. Could they hear? I wait, sweat dripping down my sides.

The voices are closer now. "I still say this is overkill, Francine," a man's voice says. "Code seventy-three is very clear. People make their own choices."

"We lost Chuck. We can't afford to lose anyone else because of them," the woman says. Francine?

Uh-oh. Chuck didn't want to talk to her on the cab radio. I don't think he trusted her.

"I just don't understand why you're devoting so much energy to tracking down a couple of kids . . ." the man says. "I saw what you did with that India. I don't think she would have made that decision without assistance."

He said India. They're talking about us.

I can see them through the locker vents now. A short woman wearing a silvery vest that glistens like a hologram. She has brown hair that swings like a pendulum when she walks and bright pink glasses. The man is in the traditional blue security outfit. Oh! It's Manny, the guy at the border crossing. I thought his voice sounded familiar.

"Don't be such a purist, Manny. She just needed a little help is all. I want to get these kids settled. The boy worries me. When was the last time Sparky offered anyone a job?"

"He's twelve, Francine," Manny says. "I don't see how he could be a threat."

"You didn't answer my question."

"I don't ever remember Sparky offering anyone a job."

"Exactly. And the little one is a loose cannon."

"C'mon, Francine, this is the natural order of things and you know it. This isn't about you and Sparky not getting along, is it?"

"Of course not. Don't be ridiculous," she scoffs. "Time is on our side, anyway. All we really have to do is throw a few obstacles in front of them."

"That isn't honoring the spirit of the law, Francine."

"You're going to report me to Headquarters? Please. All they care about is their precious vehicles. Wait, check those lockers."

Uh-oh. Our lockers?

Manny walks back to the start of the bank of

egg-shaped lockers and begins lifting the handles one by one. *Click-squeak-bang. Click-squeak-bang.* The unlocked lockers get opened and banged shut. *Clic-cric.* The locked lockers make a constricted sound.

He's almost to Mouse's now. I think I can jam the mechanism on mine, so he won't be able to open it, but Mouse won't know to do this, will she? I don't dare say anything now.

Click-squeak-bang. Manny opens and shuts the locker next to Mouse on the other side. I hold my breath, my heart beating like a basketball on pavement.

Clic-cric. Mouse's doesn't open.

I hold the lever down hard. *Clic-cric.* Mine doesn't either.

"Let's walk to the end." Francine's voice again. "Then we'll double back."

I wait for their footsteps to recede, for their voices to fade away.

"Good work jamming the locker, Mouse," I whisper when the passage is silent again except for the low rumble of the heating system.

"Can I come out now?" she asks.

"Yeah," I say, lifting the handle on my locker, only it doesn't move. I must have jammed it too hard. I wiggle it, knock it, shove my weight against it. But it won't budge. I can't get the door open.

"Finn," Mouse asks. "Can you get me out, Finn? Can you?"

CHAPTER 23
MEMORY LOCKER

I try to control the waver in my voice. "There has to be a way to spring it open," I tell her. It's dark in the locker and a tight fit. There's light in the hallway, and some filters through the vents, but not enough to see the mechanism clearly.

The lock mechanism looked like the kind they have at the Y—the ones where you bring your own lock. They shouldn't have jammed this way.

Are the hinges bent? Did we break the lock somehow? I try to kneel down so I can get a good look, but there's no room for that. The only way I fit is standing up. I let my hands be my eyes, feeling how the lock works.

My fingers explore the lever to trip the door. Why

would Mouse's locker and my locker get jammed at the same time? What are the odds of that?

"Finn," Mouse calls. "I found something. It's a sign!"

"Inside the locker? Can you see what it says?"

"How to open the locker. One: Remember what you want to forget. Two: Ask yourself a question you can't answer. Three: Remember what you wish more than anything you hadn't forgotten."

"What?"

"How to open the locker. That's what it says, Finn. Right here."

"No locker opens that way."

"Yeah, but the sign says it, Finn," Mouse says emphatically.

"How can you remember what you forgot? It's impossible. If you've forgotten it, then how can you know what it is?"

"If Bing were here, Bing would do that part. He would know what I'd forgotten that I want to remember."

I'm about to say that's crazy, but then I realize there's something to this.

"Hey, I know," Mouse says, "*you* can do that part. You can think of something that I forgot. And I have to think of something you forgot."

This is why Mouse is amazing. Just when you think she's completely Looney Tunes she comes up with something like this. "That's a good idea, Mouse!"

"Do I just say it out loud, Finn? Will the locker hear?"

"I don't see how that's possible, but let's try it."

"One: Remember what you want to forget," Mouse says. "That's easy. How much I miss Mommy. I try to forget this, but every minute I remember again."

"Good. That's good, Mouse, keep going."

"Two: Ask a question you can't answer. Why doesn't India play with me anymore?"

"That'll do," I say.

"Now you gotta help me with three. Remember what you wish you didn't forget," Mouse says.

"You never forget anything, Mouse," I mutter. But I'm six years older than she is. There has to be something I remember that she doesn't. Something when she was little maybe. "Where did the name Bing come from?"

"Bing's mom," Mouse replies.

"I don't think so. I think it came from the song India used to sing to you. Man did you love that song. B-I-N-G, B-I-N-G, and Bingo was his name-o. Remember, Mouse? Remember?"

"Finn?"

"Yeah, Mouse."

"My locker opened."

Mouse is out now. She puts her eye up close to the locker vent so she can see me inside. Her finger pokes through for a finger wave.

"You do it now," she says.

"One: Remember what you want to forget." I take a deep breath. That one isn't hard to answer. "The day Daddy died."

"Was I there?"

164

"You weren't born yet. Mommy was in the hospital. She was about to have you. I went with Grandma Essie to visit Dad."

"He was in a car accident taking Mommy to the hospital because I wanted to get out of Mommy's tummy," Mouse fills in.

"That wasn't your fault, Mouse."

"India thinks it was."

"No she doesn't. She just misses Dad like I do. Anyway, he survived the accident. He was going to be fine," I say.

"But then his heart stopped," Mouse chimes in. "So he never got to meet me."

"Grandma Essie stopped at the hospital gift shop to buy candy for the nurse who was taking care of Mommy and you in Mommy's tummy."

"Where was India?"

"With Aunt Sammy. I headed up the back stairs to Daddy's room. Grandma Essie said not to, but I couldn't wait to see him. I thought he was playing hide-and-seek under the covers. Then I thought he was sleeping. I called to him, 'Daddy wake up. It's Finn! Daddy!'"

"Did he wake up, Finn? Did he?" Mouse asks.

"No," I whisper. "He didn't."

It's quiet now. All I see is Mouse's eye pressed up close against the locker vent.

"Two: Ask a question you can't answer," Mouse prompts.

"Uh-huh," I mutter, trying to keep the waver out of my voice. "How do you grow up without a dad?"

"Don't worry, Finn," Mouse chirps, "there are books for that. Mommy will take us to the library when we get home. I get to do the last one, Finn. Remember what you didn't want to forget. What's Coach P.'s cell number?"

"Eight-oh-five, five-five-five, oh-one-oh-nine."

"Did it open? Did it?"

"That is his cell number, Mouse."

"Oh, I've got it. How old is Henry in dog years?"

"Twenty-eight. That won't work. That's right too."

"Finn," Mouse scolds, "what have you forgotten?"

"I don't know, Mouse. That's the point."

"What is Uncle Red's address?"

"Fourteen Horsehair Reservoir Road, Fort Baker, Colorado."

"Nu-uh. It's twenty-seven Horsehair Reservoir Road," Mouse cheers. "Open it now, Finn! Open it now!"

Once again I try the lever, but the lever doesn't budge. "Still locked."

"How could it still be locked?"

"Maybe because I didn't want to remember that," I mutter.

"Ohhhh," Mouse sighs.

In the silence I hear my clock ticking and Mouse's too. What if she can't think of something? What if we time out right here?

"I know," Mouse says finally. "Finn, what was it like to sit on Daddy's lap?"

I try to call this up. I want to remember what it felt like to be that safe, that loved. I want it more than anything. I can remember his face. The way he laughed. The way his eyes shone.

"I don't remember, Mouse," I say miserably as the lock mechanism clicks open.

"Finn!" Mouse is smiling now, her face lit up like a carnival ride. She wraps the fingers of her good hand around mine. "C'mon, Finn," she says, "let's go."

CHAPTER 24
THE BLUE TRAM

It seems like everything happened so fast. One minute I was in Chuck's taxi. The next minute I'm in this tram whizzing back to my welcomer station, gliding along on the cushiony blue monorail seats. Finn and Mouse will do fine without me. They stick together, those two. They don't need me to solve some puzzle about a box, that's for sure. They are better at puzzles than I am.

My wrist screen has my welcomer group on it. They are singing a new welcoming song, but there's an empty spot in row two. My spot. See, that's just like them. They saved a spot for me and I'll save one for Maddy. She'll find a way to get here. Maddy gets what she wants.

I wonder who will be arriving today. For a second I feel an aching longing for the sound of my name on the loudspeaker. India! India! There is nothing like your own welcoming.

But a welcoming like that only happens once. I know that now.

I shouldn't have made Laird mad. I will need to apologize to him first thing, I decide as the tram passes through the great entrance, which I remember from when we came through in the feather cab. *Welcome to Falling Bird,* it says in a prism of color glowing on the streets below.

The tram hums on beyond the city gates. The glass doors open, but there's no one to get in or out. The doors slide shut again and the tram zips forward. According to the map posted above my seat, the next stop is mine— the amphitheater—and from there it's a short hop by foot to my welcomer station. I scooch down the row of sky blue cushions to the glass doors, which are already opening. I'm getting up when the white cat from my dream house leaps into the tram, landing on the seat almost noiselessly. Where did she come from?

I brush past her, fur grazing my arm as I lurch toward the doorway, but the glass door slides shut, bumping me back. I flail around, grabbing for a handle to keep from falling as the tram glides on with me and the white cat inside.

What happened? Did I hesitate and lose my chance to get off? It almost seemed like the tram door closed in my face on purpose. I know what my mom would say. *Don't be a victim, India. The world is not out to get you, you made a choice.* But how could that be? I chose to get off and the cat got in my way.

Don't make tough decisions when you're upset. Wait until you're calm and you can think it all through. But I don't have that luxury here, Mom. What then?

I study the color-coded map again. There are five more stops on this line. The next one is Headquarters Bungalows. I'll get off there.

The white cat is retching. She pukes up a yellow green mess of slimy liquid on the blue cloud carpet.

"Kitty?" I call.

I don't even know her name.

She stares at me as if she knows things she doesn't want to tell. But how could she tell me anything? She's a cat. Am I losing my mind?

The tram doesn't slow at Headquarters Bungalows. I can barely read the letters on the platform as we speed by. I only recognize the stop by the blur of purple and turquoise colors on the sign. The tram rumbles in a hopeful way at Vehicle Registration. There's a small cluster of passengers waiting to board. I'm sitting in front of the doors now, so I can leap out the second they open. But the tram doesn't stop at Vehicle Registration or Weather Group Station or Awareness Training. There is only one station left. Passengers Waiting.

Passengers Waiting? That sounds lame. I hate waiting.

Still, something about this tram is creepy, and I want to get off.

When we pull up, the stop isn't outside as the others have been. The doors open into a room with glass walls, jam-packed with people. Men, women, and kids are sitting on the floor hunched over game boards, drinking sodas, lazily fanning themselves. The trash cans overflow with drink cups and empty hamburger containers.

Every chair is claimed. Almost every square foot of the floor too. These people look like they're camping out in this room. How long have they been here?

No way am I getting off. Even if the tram is creepy, it's a whole lot better than that place. The white cat is up now. She walks on stiff, uncertain legs.

The cat's weird. I don't know why she was in that perfect house with me. She was the only part that didn't totally make sense. She's a white cat with a dark side, I swear it. Now I wish she'd go away.

I stare out at the packed room as numbers are called over the loudspeaker. "Five-eight-two-two-two-one dash four-five-seven-six-seven-eight-A," the mechanized voice announces. But no person looks at his or her number. No one even listens to the numbers being called. They continue talking as if the numbers don't mean anything. Nothing at all.

If only this tram would move so I can book it back to the amphitheater and have a do-over of this lame day.

"Final stop. All passengers must disembark and take

a ticket from the dispenser located on the rear wall." The mechanical voice is closer now—it's coming through the speaker inside the tram. My scalp begins to itch, my head throbs.

"Final stop. All passengers please disembark," the voice repeats.

Mom. I need my mom. Whatever is happening here is beyond what Maddy can handle. I dig in my pocket for my cell and push the on switch, wishing so, so hard that it would connect. Mom could tell me how to get out of here. She would know what to do, but the stupid cell won't turn on.

The tram motor gears up into its about-to-move hum. I sink back into the cushion, breathing out a tiny sigh of relief. But when my back makes contact with the sleek blue cushion, a burst of turbulent air sends me flying head over heels. I grab the seat, the handle, the glass, but the air system like a mini tornado carries me and the hissing, scratching cat out the tram door and into the crowded room.

The doors of the tram slide shut and the tram glides forward.

I watch from the glass-paneled room, a ticket I don't remember taking in my hand. The tram gains speed quickly. I watch until the last car speeds by in a blue blur.

CHAPTER 25
TUNNEL DOGS

I try my best to hurry Mouse along. We lost a half hour in the lockers. We can't afford to make a mistake like that again. We don't have time to take a wrong turn either. So far there has only been one direction, but up ahead the paths diverge in all directions like the spokes of a wheel. This worries me. Plus, before you even get there, you must first pass through a door made entirely of glass.

I try the handle. Locked, of course.

It's Mouse who sees the sign. *Ticketed Passengers Only Beyond This Point.*

"Do you still have your boarding pass?" I ask.

Mouse digs in her pocket with her good hand and

fishes out her boarding stub. I find mine and together we locate the bar code reader. The red light scans the tickets and the door slides open.

On the other side, Mouse begins looking for signs to tell us which way to go, when a dog howls in the distance.

"That way!" Mouse shouts. "That's them . . . the tunnel dogs!"

It's possible there are dogs in each direction. But I can't stop Mouse now. She is half running down the center path.

And then the tunnel makes a sharp right and a solid corrugated aluminum door appears, also locked. More dogs are howling now, just beyond the door.

I smell dogs and straw and kibble and wet fur. It smells like Henry! Mouse is jumping up and down, holding her arm steady. All we have to do is open the door.

I kneel down, running my hand along the locked handle. Is there a key pad? A bar code reader? A fingerprint access? Could we jimmy the lock?

Mouse studies the corrugated door and the sleek surrounding space looking for signs.

But there are no signs; there is nothing but a small insignia of the company that manufactured the door.

"What's it say?" I ask.

"Franklin Doors," Mouse answers.

"I never heard of 'em," I mutter. "But then again, I don't know the names of any companies that make doors."

"Franklin," Mouse repeats. "Do you know anyone named Franklin, Finn?"

"There's Benjamin Franklin. And a turtle named Franklin in a book. And a president named Franklin," I say.

"A famous president?"

"All presidents are famous, Mouse," I tell her as she leans against the door and wiggles the fingers of her good hand into her shoe.

"No, Finn. Only the rich ones are famous. The ones they put on money," Mouse insists.

"The money presidents aren't rich, they're just extra-famous," I tell her as she hands me a dime.

"What's this for?" I ask.

"Which president is on there?"

I look closely at the dime. Eisenhower maybe? But wait. Could it be Franklin Roosevelt?

I inspect the mechanism under the handle again. This time my fingernail detects a small silver slot just dime-size.

I slip her dime into the slot. The coin hits the money box and the lock clicks open. "You're brilliant, Mouse," I tell her as a mechanical arm opens the door *tchk, tchk, tchk*.

Inside is an enormous room full of dogs in traveling cages—one on top of the other five pallets high. The pallets are stacked next to a series of ramps so the dogs can go up to their cages. Some crates are empty, but most have one dog inside. There are all kinds of dogs:

German shepherds, golden retrievers, Great Danes, poodles, Yorkies, corgies, and some breeds I've never even seen before.

The dogs aren't locked into their traveling crates, the doors are open. Each dog is free to go. There's even a doggy door in the back wall of the room where they could leave if they wanted, but every dog stays in its crate. The dogs sniff, their tails wag hesitantly. They're eager to check us out like people scanning the crowd for familiar faces. Once they've seen us, they settle back down again. We are not who they're waiting for.

"Look." Mouse points to a photo of a kid clipped to the front of one cage. Pictures of one kid, sometimes two or three are attached with metal clips to each crate.

"The owners . . ." I say. "That must be who they're waiting for."

Mouse surveys the great stack of dog cages. "Warrantine?" she asks.

"What?"

"What you said Henry would have to do if she flew with us."

"Oh, quarantine. . . . Maybe. Maybe they need their owners to release them."

Mouse walks from one end of the pallet to the other, inspecting the dogs. "Is anybody feeding them?"

"Must be. They seem well cared for."

Mouse points to a crate on the first tier. "What about this one?" The door is wide open, like the others, but there's no photo clipped to the front, and the big dog inside has clean bandages—like white high-top booties—on all four feet. The center of each bandage has a strip of tape decorated with a string of pink hearts. The dog—tan and black, a long-haired German shepherd with strange blue eyes and a bitten-up ear—huddles in the corner.

Mouse digs a Milk-Bone out of her pocket and breaks it in two.

"Where'd you get that?" I ask.

"From home."

"When we were trying to get Henry back in the house?"

She nods.

When was that, I wonder. Two days ago? Three?

Mouse holds up the Milk-Bone, but the blue-eyed dog continues to cower in the back, as if she can't get far enough away from us.

"How do you think she got hurt?" Mouse asks.

I shake my head.

Mouse takes a step closer. The dog doesn't move a muscle except for her blue eyes that track every move we make.

Mouse throws half the Milk-Bone into the crate and we walk up and down the pallets, wondering how we can convince a dog to come with us.

The blue-eyed dog waits until Mouse has moved to the other side of the pallet, then she swoops down on the

Milk-Bone, and dashes back to the dark corner of her crate. She watches us, her black lips holding the unchewed bone while drips of drool slide out of her mouth.

She keeps waiting, until she can't stand it anymore and crunches down on the bone. When she has licked up every crumb, she lies down again, her eyes trained on us.

Now Mouse tosses her the other half of the Milk-Bone and the dog goes through the same ritual again.

These are the tunnel dogs? How are they ever going to help us find the black box? They can't even leave their crates.

"We'll never get them to come with us."

"This one will," Mouse announces.

"She's all bandaged up, Mouse."

Mouse pushes her hair back. Her face is filthy, her hair is wildly uncombed on one side and matted down on the other. She looks even crazier than normal. "So? My arm is hurt and you don't leave me."

"The bandages are clean. Somebody's taking good care of her." The dog's ears are cocked forward like she's listening intently.

Mouse whispers to the blue-eyed dog. She appears to be explaining our situation in detail and then suddenly from the other side of the Franklin door we hear people approaching.

"They couldn't have made it this far." Manny's voice. "We would have seen them."

Uh-oh. Manny and Francine.

"Mouse," I whisper, "we've got to get out of here."

"No harm in checking." Francine booms. "Only costs a dime."

"We're not passengers, Francine. We shouldn't be in here and you know it."

"C'mon, Mouse!" I half drag her to the doggy door in the back as we hear the *tchk, tchk, tchk* of the Franklin door opening.

CHAPTER 26
PASSENGERS WAITING

There isn't enough air in this room. It's stuffy and everybody looks grimy and tired and all packed together. God, I hope I don't look like they do. But you know what? I don't even care right now. I just want to get out of here and back to the welcomer station. Laird will fix me up.

I hope they come for me soon, I think as I find a spot on the blue linoleum in the corner next to a garbage can that smells like mustard. My back is to the wall. I bury my head in my hands, ignoring everyone. Like I want to talk to any of these people?

I only lift my head when they announce a new set of numbers. Then I pull out my ticket and listen carefully to the long series of digits. Why am I the only person doing this? Do they know their numbers by heart? Even so, they'd have to listen, wouldn't they? None of these people even stop their conversations. The dude next to me sings softly to himself. He has a clock just like I do. But his doesn't seem to be moving. I pull mine out. My clock isn't moving either. It's stuck at six hours and thirteen minutes.

A little kid of six or seven is playing with a tiny plastic pig in a Superman suit. The white cat is huddled under a chair, looking hot and unhappy.

"Here kitty." But when I get close, she hisses at me. She still has my cool mom's ring around her neck, tied with a lime green bow. I can't imagine the ring isn't intended for me. My fake mom knew I liked it. She knew it made me uncomfortable too, but I might as well look at it. What's the harm of that?

I approach the cat again. This time she lets me, but her eyes are filled with scorn. Is it possible for a cat to roll her eyes? I could swear that's what she just did. Still, she seems to know I need the ring. She allows me to take it, then trots back under the chairs.

I slip the ring on my hand and admire it as I did in my totally perfect house. My eyes are caught by the light reflecting in the stone and then suddenly I'm seeing images in the crystal.... It's the Wednesday before Thanksgiving. I let myself in the back door. My mom is on the phone. She's begging some guy to let us keep the house. She sounds desperate—not like my mom at all. She has, I suddenly realize, lost her home too.

Now there's a new image in the crystal. It's December, and Maddy and I are staying up all night watching our favorite dinosaur cartoons. We are too old for this stuff, but we loved them when we were little, and now we watch when Maddy is depressed. We don't watch when I'm depressed. I'm not allowed to get depressed when Maddy's happy.

And then it's January, and Maddy is coming into the multi-purpose room when I'm rehearsing for the talent show. I'm going to sing a solo, but Maddy doesn't like this. She motions for me to come over. I excuse myself and go talk to her. She says Brendan is playing lacrosse and I need to go watch him practice because all her friends are there.

A tiny voice inside me says no. I'm not sure I even like Brendan. I always know what he's going to say and it's never very interesting. I want to be in the talent show. "C'mon, In—what's important to you? I mean seriously . . ." Maddy says.

The tiny voice inside keeps telling me to say no to Maddy, but I can't. I go with her, and Mrs. Mahoney cuts me out of the program. She only takes the kids who show up for practice. When the talent show comes, I don't go.

And then Valentine's Day and my mom is telling me her ring is missing. Mouse says Maddy took it.

Maddy would never steal anything. Mouse is a big fat liar.

Mom says I have to ask Maddy. I tell her forget it. No way. Mom says either I will ask Maddy or she will.

I won't. She does.

Maddy practically stops talking to me. She acts as if I stink like three-day-old barf. *How dare you* is all she says to me for one whole week. And then suddenly she's back acting like nothing ever happened. Later that day, I find an envelope in my backpack. Inside is the ring. Nothing else.

Now I see recent scenes in quick clips. Me being chosen for welcomer because of how well I sing. Me talking to the other welcomer girls—we are giggling and laughing—there's no one girl who has more friends than anyone else. No one girl who decides what the rest of us will do. We are all friends. It's so easy—so comfortable. Laird tells us what to do. All that's missing is Maddy.

I grab that stupid cat and tie the ring right back to her stupid ribbon around her stupid neck.

Then I get up and begin to inspect the room. There are two doors. The big glass doors where the tram deposits people, and a smaller glass door at the back. I peer through the glass in the small door, but it's smoky and I can't see through. Of course it's locked. No surprise there.

A girl who is about Finn's age is watching me. She has

freckles, serious blue eyes, and a head full of curls the color of cut mangos—a more yellowy red than Mouse's paprika-colored hair. She smiles when she sees me test the door. "New people always do that," she says.

"How do you get out of here?" I ask.

"I wish I knew. My name's Skye," she says, and waits for me to tell her mine, which I don't feel like doing. But I hear my mom's voice in my head. Just be polite whether you want to or not. "I'm India," I say.

"Hi." She smiles.

"I don't get this place. How long do you have to stay here?" I ask.

"From what I've seen, we're pretty much stuck. Everything's stuck. Even my clock has stopped ticking. What about yours?"

"Yep, mine's stopped too. Why? Why are we here?" I ask.

"We were supposed to make a decision about whether or not to become a citizen of Falling Bird, but we couldn't, so they stuck us in Passengers Waiting."

I think about this. Do I want to be a welcomer? Suddenly this seems like a totally new question, something I've never really asked myself before.

It might not be too late to change my mind. What are the consequences of my decision, that's what my mom would ask. My mom is not always wrong. She's not always right either.

Skye nods as if she understands I need time to think

about this. "Just be careful of the lady over there in the yellow hat—Phyllis," she whispers, and then walks over to talk to the little boy with the superpig.

I go back to my corner, sit on the floor with my back to the wall, and try to turn on my wrist screen. "Maddy, please, I have to talk to you about something," I whisper.

"Hey!" a woman shouts. "Where'd you get that?"

"What? What?" A man's booming voice.

"Let me see." The woman, Phyllis, dives for me, her stale milk breath in my face.

"Hey, let me!"

Other voices chime in. The shouts come from all around, closing in on me.

"You're not supposed to have that. It creates longing."

"How'd you get it?"

A bald man puts his greasy hand on my arm.

Even Skye and the singing dude are watching me now, but it isn't me they're interested in. It's the wrist screen.

"It's broken," I tell them.

Phyllis's worn brown eyes light up. "I can fix it," she announces.

"If it's broken, it's no use to you," the bald man says. "Why not give it to me."

"They don't break," someone else says. "You just don't know how to use it. I'll show you."

"Hey, me! Me!" Another guy pushes forward.

There are no officer dudes in this room. I'm on my

own here. These people are going to jump me and take this last thing, this only thing I have left. They're going to rip it off my arm.

"Maddy," I whisper to the screen. "I so need you right now."

But Maddy does not appear. The screen is blank as a closed eye.

Phyllis is now fighting off the others. "She said she's giving it to me," she cries.

"No I didn't." A voice rises inside me. A loud, sure voice. It's not me acting like a good student or a cool girl or a good welcomer or the girl Brendan has a crush on or anybody's sister. It isn't the voice of my mother or Maddy or Laird either. It isn't me pretending at all. It's the voice of India Tompkins, exactly as I am. "Get the heck away from me!"

Instantly, the bickering stops, the room is silent. Everyone watches me.

"This is mine! Leave me alone!" I shove the bald man with the greasy hands back.

That is when the loudspeaker calls another number, another number that no one has, that no one will ever have. No one needs to check their small raffle numbers. The numbers mean nothing.

"Five-four-nine-one-eight-eight-nine-eight-one-six-oh-oh-oh-five-four-one," the mechanical voice repeats.

"Hey." Skye is next to me. She whispers in my ear, "That's you."

I look down at the ticket in my hand. Five-four-nine-one-eight-eight-nine-eight-one-six-oh-oh-oh-five-four-one, it says.

Skye nods. "Go on," she tells me.

"Impossible!" a fat man bellows. "One number's off. They like to fool with us that way."

"No, it's her number. I saw," Skye insists.

"It's because of the screen," somebody shouts.

What do you do when your number is called? I stare stupidly at my ticket.

Phyllis's bulky shoulders shove in front of me. "You won't need that now." She grabs my wrist with her large man hands, works her fingers under the strap, and snaps the wrist screen off my arm.

But I am not a victim. I am not going to stay in Passengers Waiting. I am India Tompkins and I'm a fighter. I jump on her back like a mountain lion, kicking her under the arm so hard it surprises her and for a second she loosens her grip on the wrist screen. That second is all I need. I snatch it back and jerk my arm out of her reach. Skye, the singing dude, and the little boy with the superpig all cheer. Skye is holding the white cat. The cat looks different now, as if she's finally content. That's the last thing I notice when the smoked glass door slides open, and I walk through with the wrist screen in my hand.

CHAPTER 27
PERMANENT RESIDENT

A woman with blue gloves, thick shoulders, and short hair the color of white chocolate stands at the door. *Mary Carol*, her name badge reads. She checks my ticket, nods, and tells me to follow her down a long hall with corrugated aluminum walls and smooth, shiny, handle-less doors.

Where is she taking me?

I'm gripping my wrist screen so tightly my fingers ache from the effort. The band is broken, but while I'm walking I figure a way to fix it by poking another hole in the band with the buckle sprocket. It's still loose, but at least it's on now.

The doors are numbered with a strange series of letters and numbers I don't understand. E-10K-28L, one says. E-8K-14L another. At G-19K-1L, the woman stops and pushes open the smooth metal door in the corrugated wall.

The room inside is sleek and silver with shiny walls and smooth handles inlaid into the metal. The woman slides her fingers in and clicks out a handle that flips down a seat from the wall. She moves to another handle and another seat falls out. When she has four seats, a table, a drawer full of soft drinks and another of peanuts, she invites me to sit down.

"Chuck wants to see you," she explains, offering me a soft drink.

"Chuck? The taxi driver?" I ask. Somehow this seems like good news, as if Chuck is an old friend.

Mary Carol nods. "Everybody likes Chuck. We don't want to lose him. Training is expensive and even after we're done there's no guarantee we'll end up with an employee of Chuck's caliber." She sighs. "But he's become a little too personally involved this time."

She waits as if to measure my response.

"Involved with what?" I ask.

A pained smile darts across her lips. "Your family," she explains. "We need you to let him know you decided fully of your own accord. In exchange, you will be restored to your welcomer position. That's what you want, isn't it?" she asks, watching me intently.

"I decided what of my own accord?"

"To come back."

"I don't feel the same way now," I say cautiously, fishing for information.

She shrugs. "Now isn't so important."

"Why?"

She grinds her teeth. "Some decisions you don't have a chance to make again, India. They time out."

That's what happened to my mom. She made a decision about the house and she couldn't get out of it and then we ran out of time. I feel suddenly so sad for my mom. This must be how she felt.

Mary Carol watches me carefully. "But if you're caught between the two . . . which was the decision General Operations made about you . . ."

At school I don't like to ask questions. I'm afraid people will think I'm stupid. But I don't care now. I have to understand this. "What does that mean?"

"We like things to run smoothly is all. When we have someone who doesn't want to . . . settle down—a malcontent I guess you'd call it—we try to keep them away from the general population. Dissatisfaction is infectious. Of course there are pockets of discontent in every society . . . no city is perfect. But with you it was more that you didn't seem sure you wanted to give up your passenger status."

"So you put me in Passengers Waiting?"

"Yes," she says. "Passenger status is a tumultuous time. During the downward motion euphoria, our citizens generate positive feelings for the passengers.

But interaction much beyond that . . . seems to incite troubling feelings for our residents. Chuck is a perfect example."

"He is?" The Chuckinator seemed pretty mellow to me. I'm having a hard time following this.

"The *no passengers beyond this point* ruling limits our exposure, which is better for everyone."

"No passengers beyond this point," I echo. "What does that mean?"

"It means that most of Falling Bird is off limits to you until you become a citizen with a permanent passport. That way our residents have some protection."

"From us?"

She nods, scratching her short white hair with its pink scalp showing. "But we try to treat passengers fairly. We received a Form six-twenty-one on you. Contesting our ruling on your placement in Passengers Waiting. Ordinarily we might have ignored this, but since it came from Chuck—we all really like Chuck, you see?"

"Yes."

"So we need to know . . . did you make this decision of your own free will?"

My hands are shaking. I remember the path with the light that suddenly appeared. It was so enticing. But I wanted it too. I did. Was it my own free will? This isn't a black-and-white answer. Should I lie about this? What would my mom do? What would Maddy do? Maddy would lie, that's for sure.

191

"Yes, I chose," I whisper.

"All right then." Mary Carol nods encouragingly and pushes a button on the wall.

"Yes?" the voice asks.

"Send him in," Mary Carol requests.

A moment later the door slides open and a security dude with ears shaped like pork chops appears. *Boris*, it says on his cloud patch. Behind him is Chuck outfitted in an all-white flight suit.

Chuck smiles at me, though he is so nervous the smile is more of a tic.

"India?" Mary Carol asks pointedly. "Tell him what you told me."

I stare at him, suddenly so cold I'm shivering. He'll know if I gave the right answer. "I decided," I croak, scanning his eyes for a response.

Mary Carol nods her head like I should go on. "You decided *what*, India?"

"To stay here," I say. I feel a little more like myself saying this. It's as if speaking these words gives me back a flicker of the power I felt fighting for my screen in the waiting room. I'm not a victim. I told the truth just as I saw it, even if it will get me in trouble.

Boris motions for Mary Carol to step outside, to talk about something. Mary Carol shakes her head. I'm guessing leaving me alone with Chuck is against regulations.

"Oh for goodness' sake, Mary Carol. Chuck will come too," Boris says.

Mary Carol nods reluctantly, and the three of them leave me alone in the chrome-plated room.

When they come back, Mary Carol is smiling. "Congratulations, India. You've earned your welcomer job back," she announces.

"Okay, you did your bit, Chucko, time to go." Boris flaps his hand at the Chuckinator.

Chuck nods, but there's something he wants to tell me. His eyes contain a whole conversation he can't express. "Mouse wanted me to give you this." He hands me my dad's old brown wallet—now Bing's.

Bing's wallet is always with Bing. Bing is always with Mouse. It's not possible that this wallet is here with me and Mouse is not. If she's given me Bing's wallet, she's given me Bing.

Nobody could make her do that. She had to want to herself.

I want to open the wallet, but not in front of them. I slip it into my pocket as I overhear Mary Carol whisper to Boris, "You checked it, right?"

"Yes, ma'am."

"Thanks," I tell Chuck, as if this is no big deal.

He nods, his eyes on me. This time he allows Boris to hustle him outside.

Mary Carol snaps the chairs back up into the wall, closes the soda drawer and the snack drawer. The room is a sleek silver rectangle again—with no trace of the way it was with us in it. "All righty then," she says, holding the door open for me.

CHAPTER 28
BOOM

On the other side of the doggy door, my eyes adjust slowly to the dark tunnel light. The colors are different here: every shade of brown, but no bright colors, nothing vibrant.

The passageway is expertly dug and surprisingly clean, though it's made of dirt. There's a sheen to the tunnel walls, a deep brown glow—as if the dirt has been polished. Not much space down here though. The tunnel is just dog-size—no way for us to move through except on our hands and knees, which is hard on Mouse since she can't use one of her arms.

When we get some distance from the tunnel dogs—

far enough that it feels safe to whisper—we stop and regroup.

Mouse watches me as I pull out my clock. "We can't leave without the dog, no matter what time it is," Mouse insists. "Chuck said."

"He didn't say we had to. He said it would be helpful."

"We can't leave the dog," Mouse says, stubbornly.

We have to go back, figure out a way to avoid Francine and Manny, persuade a dog to come with us, and find India and the black box all in five hours and nineteen minutes. How is this possible?

"Remember the time Henry ran away, Mouse? Remember how we got her back?" I ask.

"She followed you."

"She was running toward TO Boulevard and I ran the other direction. She turned around and began chasing after me, remember?"

"You think the blue-eyed dog will follow us?"

I nod.

"What if Francine locks her in?"

I hadn't thought of that. "She won't do that, Mouse," I lie.

"You promise, Finn?" she whispers hopefully. "Pinkie swear?"

I don't answer this.

Mouse nods as if no answer is her answer. She takes out her clock and looks at it. For the first time, she seems to really understand what is at stake here.

"What about you, Finn? You won't leave me, will you?" Her voice squeaks.

"I won't leave you, Mouse." I put my hand on her messy hair head. "That I can promise. Now c'mon." I try to make my voice more upbeat than I feel. "We can do this."

The farther we move into the tunnel, the closer the weather outside sounds. It's raining out there, maybe hailing too, and the wind is howling.

What is my plan B? How will we find the black box without the acute hearing of a dog? Somebody in Falling Bird must know where it is, but who?

A thunderous boom crashes overhead. The sound reverberates through my legs as the ceiling collapses, spilling soil down all around me.

Dirt pours down my chest. Weighs down my head. Goes up my nose, burns my eyes. Dirt in my mouth, in my throat.

Everything is dirt. Dirt everywhere.

Air. I need air.

I cough, try to breathe.

The shale is loose. Dark all around. Can't grasp, can't claw. I fight, dig my way out, but which way is out?

Need air.

I shove my hand up as far as it will go. One finger wiggles free. Shove, push through, now my head. Get my head up there.

I breathe great gasps of air.

Air is the best thing ever. Better than chocolate, better than basketball.

I cough the dirt out of my mouth, my nose, my throat, and then it hits me . . . Mouse? Where's Mouse? The avalanche filled the tunnel like water pouring into a glass. I can't see her anywhere.

I dig hard one way and hard the other.

Where have I searched already? Where do I need to look?

"Mouse! Mouse!" My voice is hoarse from dust and from screaming. And then suddenly I hear a whimper.

I stand stock-still to locate the sound. Left. It's coming from my left. I dig left crazy hard.

The sound is clearer now. A muffled whine, a tan paw. The blue-eyed dog is covered in dirt, her tail pinioned by a boulder the size of a basketball. I shove the boulder with my hands, heave my shoulder into it. The dog yelps as it rolls off her tail.

"Mouse!" I tell her. "Find Mouse!"

The dog begins digging one way, while I dig the other. She is a digging machine, this dog.

"Mouse!" I call, shale sifting through my fingers, dumping a fresh avalanche on my head.

And then from down the tunnel I hear a low howl and Mouse's whispered voice. "Dog. You're here."

It takes me a while to make my way through the piles of dirt, shale, rocks, and sand, but when I get to Mouse, the blue-eyed dog has her nose up close to

Mouse's grimy face, allowing herself to be petted at last.

"Are you okay?" I ask.

Mouse nods, tears making clean pink lines through the grime on her cheeks. "Finn," she says. "The dog is here."

I gulp the air, my insides rising up, filling my chest.

"You saved Mouse," I tell the blue-eyed dog, running my fingers over her thick dirty coat.

"Know what I just figured out, Finn?" Mouse asks.

"What?" I scratch behind the dog's ears.

"*Dog* is *god* backward," she says.

"We need to give her a name," I say.

Mouse puts her index finger to her chin, her head steady, her eyes looking up. "Boom," she answers. "After the sound that brought us together."

"All it took was an avalanche," I say.

Boom wags her tail.

INDIA

CHAPTER 29
WELCOMER STATION

I hang back, wanting to look in Bing's wallet, but Mary Carol has a hawk eye—she doesn't seem to mind that I'm lagging behind, but she won't let me out of her sights either. How am I ever going to get time on my own? And then it hits me. It's so obvious. Why didn't I think of it before?

"Umm, Mary Carol, I need to use the bathroom."

"Oh yes, of course," Mary Carol mutters. "Closest facility is this way." She changes course, walking back down the corridor in the direction we came and stopping at a sleek door. She presses her thumb against it and the door opens to a one-stall bathroom—no bigger than an airplane toilet—made entirely of metal.

Good. There's only room for one person.

I walk in, move the door slot to lock, which makes the light flicker on. Then I take the wallet out of my pocket.

Inside is one dollar, and the license for Bing hand-drawn by Mouse. I take it out of the plastic sleeve Mouse made from a Baggie. Tucked in another slot is something else folded and folded again—a photo of our family. My father's arm is around me and my mom. My mom's arm is around Finn. My mom is very pregnant. She looks like she might tip over, her stomach is so big.

I'm in there. Mouse has written on the side with a big arrow directed at my mom's tummy. On the back, she wrote: *Thank you, Bing, for taking this picture when I couldn't see on account of the skin.*

I can't stop staring at the photo. I've never seen it before. Mouse must have found it in the move.

My dad's smile shines out of the picture, his eyes full of love for our family. He's sure that we will stay this way forever. He doesn't know that a few weeks or maybe days later he'll be gone.

Mouse never knew him. She never felt my father's love. She never saw us when we were complete. Is that why she made up Bing?

But the moment this photo was taken my daddy loved me with all his heart. He totally did.

This is my family. Nothing in the world is more important than that.

"India." Mary Carol knocks on the door. "You're over reg time for a bathroom visit."

There's a reg time for a bathroom visit? Jeez. "Just a minute," I call, flushing the toilet.

I check to see what else is in the wallet. That's when I find the tiny slip of paper written in a handwriting I don't recognize.

India,

Sparky has your back.

Chuck

Sparky? That's the Century Training dude who's in dispatch, right? How's he going to help me? I don't even have a car.

"India." Mary Carol bangs on the door.

How much time do I have?

My clock is ticking again. I can feel it. My hand presses up against the smooth clock face. I pull it out and steal a glance . . . four hours and twelve minutes left.

I can make another choice. It isn't too late. I'm going to find Mouse and Finn. Get out of my way. I am totally doing this. I open the bathroom door.

I feel so sure and then an instant later I'm not sure again. How can I do this? I'm not smart enough to figure this out.

Wait, though. Step by step I can think it through.

I could try to get Mary Carol on my side. Chuck jeopardized his job to help us . . . would Mary Carol? She isn't mean, and she likes me. But rules are so important to her. I don't think she would break a rule for me.

We walk down the corrugated aluminum hall, going in the opposite direction from Passengers Waiting. I fall behind Mary Carol. She glances back at me, but I continue to walk, my head low, trying to adopt the most obedient posture I can muster.

I can do this. I can figure it out.

We get on another tram—the purple line. This one has a bunch of people in different Falling Bird uniforms. This tram seems more normal—but very lavendery, as if I'm in lavender land.

Mary Carol smiles at me. "You'll be a good welcomer, India. Such a beautiful voice. I'm glad we have you back."

I put on my good welcomer face, smile, and nod.

"Laird's a bit on the temperamental side," she confides in me. "You've got some apologizing to do. He'll expect you to eat crow for a while."

I nod, trying to appear engaged with Mary Carol as I figure out my plan.

Mary Carol will probably hand me off to Laird at the amphitheater. If I'm to escape, I will need to get away now or else wait until she drops me off. Waiting will take precious time, but it's less risky. It's wild in the amphitheater during a welcoming. With so many people going wild over the new arrival, it will be easier to slip away. Laird won't watch me as closely as Mary Carol does. Mary Carol's eyes are totally glued to me right now.

According to the laminated map on the wall, the ride to the checkpoint station is short. I have to get on the green line and then I could totally make it out there in time. But how will I find Finn and Mouse once I get to the checkpoint? And how will we find the black box? I don't let myself think about this. First things first.

Mary Carol notices I'm studying the map. She seems pleased to see my interest and begins explaining the different routes. I'd like to ask how you get on the green line, but I can't think of a reason a welcomer would need to know that.

It takes thirteen minutes to get to the amphitheater stop. Thirteen whole minutes. When the lavender tram slows and the glass doors slide open, I smile and wave at Mary Carol, hoping she'll trust me to find my post on my own. Fat chance. Mary Carol is in lockstep with me, marching me to my station, where Laird is in high energy mode, his hands gesturing wildly as he gives the dos and don'ts to a new recruit.

The girls see me first. "India!" They rush over, enveloping me in a big warm hug, placing my tunic over my head. When they finally let me surface again, I see Laird and Mary Carol watching me.

"Well, well, well," Laird says in an acid voice. "If it isn't India Tompkins back from the—"

"Laird," Mary Carol snaps.

Laird and Mary Carol exchange a look. "I didn't expect to see you again," Laird tells me. His voice is measured now, controlled.

"Hi, Laird," I say.

"*Hi, Laird,*" he imitates. "Surely you can do better than that, India." He waits.

"I'm sorry," I say. Am I sorry? No, not a bit. But I need to play along here. "I didn't realize how much this job meant to me."

Mary Carol clears her throat. "Statute forty-one-ninety-two," she reminds Laird, "expressly prohibits requiring wayward recruits to grovel."

Laird snorts. "I just want a decent apology, but never mind. We'll do it your way, Mary Carol. Come, India." He opens his arms as if to give me a big exaggerated hug.

Mary Carol watches this. She seems reluctant to turn me over to Laird. Clearly I am right about her. In her own procedure-bound way she likes me.

"Really, Mary Carol." Laird's eyes bug out at her. "You can go."

Mary Carol nods. She allows herself a little smile. "Nice to have you back, India," she says before disappearing into the crowd, which is bursting with welcoming fever.

Laird directs his total attention on me. "India, really, you'll need to do something with your hair," He produces a hairbrush and hands it over as he launches into a canned lecture on what he calls re-treads—people who have to go through the training a second time. Clearly I'm not the only welcomer to have deserted her post.

"Should you make the wrong choice again, India . . .

INDIA!" Laird shouts. "You're not listening to me. What did I just say?"

"Should you make the wrong choice again," I offer, but my hands are trembling. He saw that my mind was elsewhere. He suspects something.

Laird's blue eyes get small as nail heads. "How long were you in Passengers Waiting?" he asks.

"I dunno," I whisper, cold sweat dripping down my back.

"Never seen anyone get out of there." He pauses to let this sink in. "Course, you do look like something the cat dragged in, but never mind. You'll stay with me today, and tonight we'll get you cleaned up."

My eyes are drawn to the screens, which are filled with the face of a strikingly beautiful dark-skinned boy.

"He's incredible, isn't he?" Laird's voice is gentle.

"Yes," I say truthfully.

"All right then." He smiles, his face softening.

He knows there's nothing like a handsome new welcomee to keep the welcomers happy.

CHAPTER 30
RED ALERT

I watch the movie clips of the newcomer as he wins a tennis match and reads a book to his blind sister. It feels so nice to just stand here and watch him. He is way over the top cute.

But this won't last. I know it won't.

In my hand is Bing's wallet. The one that used to be my dad's. The photo of my parents is tucked inside. They are my family. *They* are real.

I look at Laird, who is as transfixed by the screen as everyone else. Then I pull myself away from the newcomer's beautiful face radiating from the screen and I slip through the crowd. No one sees me. They are all watching the boy.

I pretend to be a runner welcomer, edging toward the road. It's a different job, with a different uniform, but in the thrill of the welcome, I am hoping no one will notice.

My plan is to take the tram to the border crossing, but when the newcomer's feather taxi drives by, I have a better idea and I take off after the car.

I've never driven a car before, but I drove a golf cart in Palm Springs when I went on vacation with Maddy's family. Her dad let us drive the cart at night when the golfers had all gone home. A car can't be much different, right?

I have no idea how I will get the car away from the taxi dude. I'm trying to work this out when suddenly Laird appears. His steely fingers wrap around my tunic. But I duck out of it, leaving my tunic in his hands. I've still got my clothes underneath. I'm totally me inside.

I take off, running so hard my whole body vibrates, but Laird's feet pound after me.

"You'll never make it, India!" he shouts.

I practically fly over the road, dodging people, weaving around groups, around carts, under banners, diving under one lady's arm. My chest heaves, my throat hurts, but I can't stop.

The cab pulls up to a house with a large elm tree and a rope swing and a stream flowing right in front of it. The driver gets out to unload the luggage, but the newcomer is too much of a gentleman to let anyone wait on him. He flashes a smile so bright I can't take my eyes off

207

of his full lips. His eyelashes are so lush and long they seem unreal.

He's joking with the driver. I lean closer to hear what they're saying as they unload together. He's so relaxed, so confident, the kind of person everybody likes to hang with, the kind of person who has his own thoughts, the kind of person who says things you don't expect.

I could talk to him . . .

But then all at once I understand. I don't want a piece of someone else's life . . . I want my own. I want my chance to live my own life my own way.

I leap forward and slip into the driver's seat. When the driver reaches up to shut the trunk, I pounce on the gas pedal and the feather taxi shoots forward, veering wildly onto the sidewalk. I forgot I have to steer and press the gas pedal at the same time. I get a firm grasp on the wheel and manage to turn the car so it thumps back over the curb and onto the street.

The driver is running after me, waving his short arms. I drive onto the sidewalk on purpose this time to avoid the crowds in the street. Once I've made it past the amphitheater, I press the accelerator pedal as far as it will go and fly down the almost deserted street. I look back but the driver is so far behind he'll never catch up.

Mary Carol totally explained the map to me. I was thinking I'd be on a tram, but the route is almost the same. I know how to get to the inspection station.

What I don't know is how long it will take the

driver to alert the blue security dudes. Can they see the taxi on a radar screen? Am I being watched now? The only people here are clustered around the screens. They aren't looking at me. But what about the people in Headquarters—the people who run Falling Bird, can they see me?

The driver has left his jacket with *Travels with Ed* embroidered on it and his cap on the seat next to me along with his paste-on sideburns and beard. I wiggle into the jacket, switching hands on the steering wheel, then use my elbows while I wind my hair up and quickly smash the hat on, catching the wheel again with both hands.

Yes! I am so good at this!

For a few minutes I get caught up in the sheer power of being behind the wheel on the open highway. Driving is so cool! I'm glad I got to try it while there's still time. "Shut up," I tell myself. "You're so totally a fighter, India Tompkins. You can figure this out."

"Come in, number seventy-seven," a woman's voice on the radio blares. "You are making an unauthorized city exit. Please return your vehicle to the garage and report to Vehicle Registration Group. Come in, seventy-seven. It is against regulations to tamper with a vehicle. Please access your radio. We are contacting Human Behavior Group."

I pull the clock out of my pocket and glance at it. I have three hours and eighteen minutes. I can do anything in three hours and eighteen minutes, right?

I grab the radio and switch it off. The car shudders as I floor the gas pedal again.

"In, it's me! Where have you been?"

Ohmygod! Maddy is on my wrist screen, which has flipped upside down on my arm. I wiggle it around to where I can see the curly hair and sweet eyes of Maddy, my best friend.

"Maddy." The tears stream down my face. "I miss you," I sob.

"Well, come back then, In."

"I can't."

"Sure you can. I'll meet you at Laird's station."

Wait. How would Maddy know about Laird? I didn't tell her about him, did I? Is this even Maddy?

"Maddy," I whisper as the checkpoint station comes into view in the distance. The gates are closed. The golf carts are parked helter-skelter. "Talk me through this, okay?"

ALL PASSENGER VEHICLES PLEASE SLOW FOR INSPECTION, a sign reads.

"I don't want to go back there, Maddy. And my clock is running out."

"Don't sweat it, In. It's all good," Maddy says.

The video screens are like great dancing billboards, like huge cineplex-size TV screens flashing: RED ALERT! RED ALERT! CAB #77 INDIA TOMPKINS.

I'm close enough to hear the speaker system droning in that mechanical voice. "Human Behavior Group is requesting the immediate return of India Tompkins. All

210

Border Group personnel please be aware of a possible vehicle theft. Suspect age fourteen, five foot one, long brown hair."

"I'm driving right into this, Maddy."

"Just be like, I'm sorry, officer, I didn't know."

"Wait, that's not true. I do know . . . just like I know you took the ring."

"What is the big deal about that stupid ring? I was going to put it back, if everybody hadn't totally freaked about it."

"If you were just borrowing it, why didn't you ask?"

"I just forgot. Man, you better be careful, you're starting to sound like Rules, India."

"You're wrong about that, Maddy. I don't sound like my mother, I sound like me," I tell her, and then all at once I want Maddy to disappear. I can't think with her talking to me this way.

And as surely as if I switched an off button the wrist screen fades gray, flickers green, and flashes off.

Okay, you've got to think this out, I tell myself. If I try to lie my way through the checkpoint, I'm toast. I'll never make it. They'll send me back to Passengers Waiting. I can't let that happen. Mouse and Finn are on the other side.

I pull off the highway and drive parallel to the wall, hoping to spot a break. But the wall goes on forever. Mile after mile of shiny aluminum, rounded at the top and three or maybe four stories tall.

I make a U-turn and head back across the road to the

other side, but it's the same thing in this direction—just wall as far as I can see. Even if I could manage to climb over, they'd see me, plus, I'd be on foot. How would I ever find Finn and Mouse on foot?

Then I see a lone cart moving along the wall. It pulls behind the tram stop. The driver leans out, pulls a lever, and a small gate opens. The cart scoots through and the gate shuts behind it, but the opening is too small for the feather cab—it's cart-size.

Here comes another cart with a young girl driving. I grab the paste-on sideburns and stick them on, jump out of the feather cab, and tear across the grass waving my arms. "Wait!" I shout.

She comes to a whiplash halt, and I jump into the passenger side.

"Hey," I say, deepening my voice as if I'm the driver, Ed. "Hi!"

She takes me in warily, snapping her gum. The name on her badge says *Pamela*. "Where's your cab—" she asks.

"I parked it already."

"You *parked* it?"

Oops. Guess I'm not supposed to have done that. If I backtrack and launch into another story, that will be worse. I keep going.

"Yeah, sure. You just have to know how." I try for a swagger.

Pamela gives me another once-over. She clearly isn't buying this. Then her eyes light on my wrist screen.

"Wow. I've never seen one of those. They're really rare. Only Headquarters people are supposed to have them. Is yours free roaming or does it have a chip?" she asks.

"A chip?"

"It allows Headquarters to alter the information."

"Oh. I don't know," I say truthfully.

She wants the wrist screen as much as the people in Passengers Waiting. I can see it in her eyes. "Yeah, check it out," I say, directing all my attention toward the screen. I know how to do this now. I can turn it on with my mind. I focus on Maddy and how much I like to talk to her. The dull gray flickers tentatively and Maddy pops up.

"In, don't do that again. I hate when you shut me out like that." Maddy has that peeved look on her face.

Pamela's riveted to the screen. "Who's that?" she asks.

I smile at Maddy. But something inside me has changed.

"My friend, when I lived in California," I say.

"Can I see?" Pamela asks, her voice suddenly vulnerable, needy.

"Sure," I say, "if I can, um, borrow your cart."

Pamela's eyes snap back to me. "You're that girl they're looking for." She snatches the radio on her dashboard and pulls the curly cord toward her.

"No! Wait!" I plead.

She freezes, her finger hovering over the transfer button.

I unbuckle the half-broken strap. "You take it. Go

ahead. There must be someone you want to talk to . . ."

"In! What are you doing?" Maddy's face is pale; her hazel eyes fill the screen, but as it moves away from my skin, wavy lines disrupt the picture.

"Bye, Maddy," I whisper as Pamela buckles the screen onto her own wrist and in place of Maddy's ghosted image comes a new face, sharply in focus. It's a pale boy with eyes an unnatural shade of blue, a thin face full of dark shadows, and the beginning of a beard.

"Pamela," he says in a thick Australian accent. "I never thought I'd see you again."

"Jack. Oh Jack," she says, her throat full, her eyes captivated. The radio falls from her hands as she strokes the screen with the tips of her fingers.

Slowly, I move my hand to the transmission stick. Then in one fierce motion, I bump Pamela out of the driver's seat, switch the transmission to drive, and pounce on the gas pedal. The cart lurches forward, I grab the wheel and sit down.

I'm surprised how easy this is. Pamela is so distracted, she pops right out of the seat into the grass.

"Sorry!" I call over my shoulder, but in the rearview mirror I see Pamela does not look up, so intent is she on her conversation with Jack.

The cart doesn't go as fast as the cab and it hits the ruts with twice the force, but I push the accelerator hard, clamping down on the wheel to keep on course. When I get to the gate lever, I scoot in close, barely skimming the handle with my fingertips, and the gate opens.

"Finn, Mouse! I am so gonna be there!" I say as the road dips and the cart goes through the gate. On the other side of the thick aluminum wall, the weather turns instantly stormy, the sky strangely blue. I begin trembling so violently I can hardly hold the steering wheel. I don't know if this is because it's freezing cold out here or because I now know for certain I can't go back. No one can help me now. I have nothing but me . . . me and my two-hour-and-twelve-minute life.

CHAPTER 31
PERIPHERY ROAD

Boom is like our own personal bulldozer. She digs a path for us out of the landslide and up to open ground in minutes.

Above ground, the cold hits like we've walked into a deep freeze. The wind bites through me. My teeth chatter. The thunder and lightning have stopped, but the rain is misting down, melting the dirty crust of snow.

I can see the border station from where we are, and the vehicles parked there. We will need one with a heater and lots of gas. I don't know if the airport is twenty minutes away or six hours. I look down at my own clock, which says one hour, fourteen minutes.

"Mouse, let's go closer, but we have to sneak," I say,

eyeing Boom. How do you tell a dog to keep her mouth shut?

This side of the border isn't manned the way the other side is. It's much plainer over here. More like Colorado must be, with meadows partially covered in snow in some spots, brown and muddy with rain in others. But there's certain to be some kind of electronic surveillance system.

Up ahead I see a lot filled with maybe fifty Segways parked in neat rows. A whole parking lot full of vehicles—though not the kind with heaters, that's for sure. Still, the keys to each are dangling from the handlebars like invitations. A sign posted to the fence says: SEGWAY USE FOR AIRPORT RETURN ONLY.

Looking better all the time.

We walk closer to the Segways and a recorded message starts playing with instructions. "First make a selection, then place the key in the ignition."

It doesn't seem too difficult. Mouse could probably manage. She follows instructions well, but how will we get Boom on board?

"Finn!" Mouse whispers.

"And when you get to the airport," the voice continues, "follow signs for the periphery road/airport return. Just remember"—the voice drops low and begins speaking quickly now like a commercial for medicine required to state the side effects—"no standing or stopping at the curb. No passenger pickup. Only one driver allowed on each vehicle and no exit from the periphery road."

Wait . . . no exit from the periphery road? My mind flashes on the first night at the airport. What was it Chuck said about the Segway riders? *They're always here.* So people just go around and around the airport waiting for planes that never arrive?

"Finn, look!" Mouse calls again, pulling on my arm. She points to an approaching girl—not much older than I am.

We dive behind a storage bin. Boom follows us. She seems to understand we are hiding and curls in a tight ball.

From here, we can watch the girl, without her seeing us. Her hair is hanging limp and wet. She's wearing a lime green Falling Bird vest and she has a wrist screen attached haphazardly to her arm.

The way she steps, her eyes in constant motion like a surveillance camera, makes me think she's not supposed to be here. She moves stealthily from Segway to Segway until she hops on the one she wants and turns the key. She has trouble with reverse—clearly she hasn't driven one of these things before. She's close to us now—very close—I can just make out the name on her shirt: *Pamela.*

Pamela manages reverse now, but it isn't pretty. She stops and starts, jerking her way out of the parking lot, and then zips forward so fast her hat flies off.

Before I can stop her, Mouse darts out. She snatches the hat and something else that's fallen too. A purse or fanny pack maybe? But when Mouse returns, I see it's the wrist screen. Mouse hands it to me.

India really liked hers—she was so secretive about it, though. I have no idea how it works. I'm about to put it in my pocket—we don't really have time to mess with this right now—when suddenly the screen lights up with a face I recognize, but don't know very well. It's a man about my father's age with a short red beard, red curly hair, and kind blue eyes.

Uncle Red.

"Finn." Uncle Red smiles as if he wants to say something important but doesn't know how to start. "I don't have kids. I didn't know myself how much I wanted them till I started talking to your mother about you all moving up here. It means a lot to me to have this chance to be a part of your lives.

"I'm looking forward to you and your sisters living up here more than I've looked forward to anything in a good long while . . . and I've been trying to figure out how to make you feel welcome. Got a hoop up already. The regulation kind. Your mom let me know you were particular. Talked to the school about getting you on the team too. The coach said he might have a spot . . ."

"Finn! Finn!" Mouse shouts. "C'mon! We've got to go."

When I look up, I see three Falling Bird security guys in their midnight blue uniforms running toward us.

INDIA

CHAPTER 32
PROPERTY OF FB

I've gotten pretty far, but now I'm not sure whether to stay on the main road, which is smoother, so I can get the cart going full speed, or go on the side roads, where I'll have to go slower because of the bumps.

I've just decided to play it safe and take the side road when the radio buzzes.

"Two-oh-two, come in, two-oh-two."

My eyes find the registration for the cart while still holding tight to the steering wheel. The road is full of potholes. It's hard to keep in control bouncing over them. The registration has that girl Pamela's picture and the vehicle number 202. Pamela was really into that Jack dude on my wrist screen. I wonder if she even called in her missing cart. I'm guessing she didn't. Should I answer and pretend to be her?

I grab the radio, take a deep breath, and push the receiver button. "This is two-oh-two," I say.

"Francine here. Our board is showing you're taking the vehicle out of your designated area."

"Oh yeah, um . . . I'm having mechanical difficulties . . . with the brakes . . . they aren't, um, working." Screwed to the dashboard of the cart is the same brass plate that is in the feather cabs. *Property of FB*, it says.

"And you didn't call in?" Francine's tone is suddenly suspicious.

"I'm going too fast. Can't take my hands off the wheel."

"Oh, of course." Francine's voice softens. "I'll patch in Mechanical Group," she says.

Wait. What did Chuck's note say? Wasn't he talking about that dispatcher dude? "Is Sparky there? He's helped me with this, um, problem before," I say.

"This isn't Sparky's area, Pamela. You should know that," Francine snaps.

Oh great. I blew that. How am I going to get her to put Sparky on?

What would a Falling Bird person do, I wonder, and then all of a sudden I know. I clear my throat. "Code eight-one-seven-two, Francine. Type two mechanical problems go to Sparky," I bluff, and then I hold my breath.

"Eight-one-seven-two. Who even *reads* the eight thousands?" Francine grumbles.

"Rules are important, Francine," I tell her.

"All right, all right. I catch your drift. I'll put him through, though there are probably three people in all of Falling Bird who have read the eight-thousand codes."

Mom, if you could only see me now. Mouse is not your only smart daughter!

"Sparky here." A man's voice comes on as my cart hits a rut, jerks left, and teeters precariously, almost flipping over.

I gasp.

"Sure you don't want me to call Mechanical Group?" Francine's voice again. Man, does she have to stick her nose in everything?

"Sparky, the brakes don't work. Remember how you helped me with this before?"

"I'll give you three minutes, then I'm patching in Mechanical," Francine says.

Her radio clicks off. I take a deep breath. "Sparky," I whisper. "I'm India Tompkins. Chuck said you would help me."

The line crackles with static. I hold my breath.

"Pamela, yes. Been tracking you and the others. Slip it in neutral, pull the emergency, and give the accelerator a whack from the side. Remember how we did it before?"

He's covering for me. He's going to help.

"I'm with you, Pamela," he says.

222

"Where are the others?" I ask as I maneuver the cart around a huge pothole and over a rocky patch, the steering wheel vibrating in my hands.

"Don't panic. Get the vehicle under control, then you can double back."

Double back? Wait. Is this a trick? Chuck said to trust this guy, and Chuck stuck his neck out for us. But still, double back?

"For the others?" I whisper.

"Yes," he says. "It's not far. If you can't unjam the brake system, we'll have someone meet you at the border crossing."

"At the border crossing?"

The line clicks on again and Francine is back. "Status, please?" she demands.

"We got the situation under control here, Francine."

"If you got the problem solved, why are you still on the horn? I'm patching in Mechanical."

"On the horn, Francine? You been skipping CA again?"

"Sorry, sorry, on the *line*," she answers.

"Mechanical Group." A new voice breaks into the line. "I understand two-oh-two is having a problem with the braking system."

"Uh-huh," I say, "the pedal was stuck. But I think I got it now. Sparky figured it out."

"All righty. Got you headed home on our screen too. Be sure to fill out Form one-one-five-one when you return. We'll get that vehicle serviced ASAP."

"Yes, sir," I say as I see the border station and a knot of people up ahead.

Ohmygod . . . it's Mouse and Finn and a dog—hey, didn't Mouse say we needed a dog?—and uh-oh, three security guys. That can't be good.

"Help! Help! Help!" I toot the horn, jam my hand on it. "I can't stop this thing!" I shout, heading straight for them, my foot hovering over the brake pedal.

When they see me coming they scatter. Finn, Mouse, the dog, and one security guy on one side, the other two uniforms on the other.

I turn toward Finn and Mouse, then pounce on the brakes. "GET IN!" I shout, and Mouse and Finn dive into the back, the dog leaping after them.

It takes the tall security guy a second to realize what's happening, but I have the pedal to the metal by then.

He's running, though, and he must be some kind of distance runner, because boy is he fast. "That's Falling Bird property!" he shouts.

"Faster!" Mouse yells.

The cart vibrates like a coffee grinder. "I'm trying!" I shout. But with two more people and a dog on board it just won't go as fast as it did.

I try my best to steer around the potholes. Between the extra weight and the rough road, the security guy is gaining on us. His long arm grabs the backseat, dragging our cart until it is hardly moving at all.

But the dog sees him now. Her teeth bared, her hackles up, she dives for his hand.

Surprised, the tall guard lets go and our cart shoots forward, unencumbered again.

"Way to go, India! Yay, Boom!" Finn and Mouse cheer as the radio buzzes urgently now and there's a distant sound of choppers in the air.

"India! India!" Mouse shouts through the buzzing, whirring noise. "Don't ever leave us again."

CHAPTER 33
THE BLACK BOX

INDIA! India came back and she brought Bing, just like Finn said she would. I want to hug her in the big Mommy way, but she is busy driving the mini car with no doors. She's wearing her hair up in Chuck's driver's cap and she has on his jacket too, only it says *Travels with Ed*. Who is Ed?

She doesn't have her driver's license yet. She's not old enough. That's why those Marvins got mad. India is a good driver, though. India is good at everything. She is a perfect big sister. Except all the time she isn't.

Bing, India, Finn, Boom. I count on my fingers. All we need now is Mommy!

The black box is how we get to Mommy. Chuck said.

We have to find the box before the helicopters land. I hear them up in the sky.

"Mouse!" India shouts. "Ask Bing where to find the black box."

Bing? She wants to know what Bing thinks?

I ask Bing and he tells me too. Does India really want to hear what Bing has to say?

"India, you got to promise to believe him," I shout.

"I will, Mouse. I promise."

"What about Mommy's ring? You didn't believe him about that."

She is silent. Just driving. "Yeah, I did, Mouse. Who do you think put the ring back for Maddy?"

I try to puzzle this out. It makes no sense to me, so Bing has to explain it. "Sometimes," Bing says, "people get more mad at you when you're right than when you're wrong."

"India, don't be mad anymore, okay, please, India, please?"

"I'm not, Mouse. I couldn't be mad at Maddy, so I got mad at you. I'm sorry. I won't let that happen again."

"India?"

"Yeah, Mouse."

I look down at my clock. "If we don't see Mommy again, will you be my mommy? I don't want a stranger mom, even if she's nice."

"Mouse, look at me." India is holding the wheel so tightly her hands are white. The air blows her hat off now as the helicopters land. "We're going to do this.

We'll get back to Mommy. But I need your help. Do you know how we can find the black box?"

"Bing says to ask Finn's little screen."

"What little screen?" India's eyes dart back to Finn.

Finn slips it out of his pocket.

"No way! I can't believe you have a wrist screen!" India shouts.

"How do I make it work? It doesn't do what I want it to," he says.

"It calls up what you want the most. Just look into it and think about the black box."

Finn's face is whiter than his arms. He whisks the hair out of his eyes and looks into the tiny screen. "Where's the black box? The black box?" he says.

Nothing happens.

"What does the black box mean to you?" India asks Finn. "Why do you want it?"

Finn looks at India like she's crazy, but he puts his mouth close to the screen and says, "Inside the black box is my own room, my own bed, my basketball, my mom, a hot shower, chocolate chip cookies, my playlist, my future, and Uncle Red."

Suddenly the screen lights up with a picture as clear as our TV. It shows a bright orange box in a junkyard.

"India, it's orange!" I yell so she can hear.

"It's okay, Mouse," Finn says. "I saw a program once. The black box is always orange."

"Where is it?" India shouts.

"In a junk pile," Finn answers.

"Ask it where."

"How will it know?" I ask as the screen starts to talk like Jimmy's mommy's car when we went on that field trip. "Prepare to turn left," the voice in the little screen says.

"It has a GPS!" Finn shouts.

Helicopters have landed near us, but the screen is in Finn's hand. It's telling us where to go.

CHAPTER 34
FIREBALL

R ight turn in fifty feet," the calm authoritative voice of the GPS tells us, oblivious to the helicopters all around.

I'm looking at the speedometer on the cart when my eyes suddenly register the brass plate on the dashboard: *Property of Falling Bird.*

"Abandon the cart," I tell India. "That's what they want, not us."

"We need it. We can't walk that far."

"Left turn in ten feet," the GPS commands.

The clock is ticking. I have thirty-nine minutes left. Mouse and India have more. We don't have time for this and then suddenly: "You have arrived at your destination."

Boom shoots out of the cart and scrambles up the hillside, where the cart can't go.

"C'mon!" I say, and we all jump out, leaving the vehicle.

Boom is running so fast, it's all we can do to keep pace. We're headed into the wind. Mouse is staying with Boom. India is close behind. It's me who can't keep up.

My legs aren't working. There's a disconnect between my head and my feet. My head is telling my feet to run, but my feet can't hear.

Inside I'm running like crazy, but my body feels heavy, like my legs are thick bags of sand. My eyelids are magnets. My body is shutting down, quitting out.

My teeth aren't chattering. I'm not warm or cold. I can't feel my chest. The urgency of the clock ticks on in my mind, but my mind can't control my body. The ticking is comforting like a lullaby; a clock singing for me. My mind is fighting to get control, but everything is slipping away.

"C'mon, Finn!" India shouts in my ear. "We can't do this without you."

"Finn," Mouse calls, her voice soft as if it's penetrating acres of gauze. Minutes go by or maybe they don't. I can't tell. The minutes are floating around me. The clock is still ticking, but I can't move anymore. Boom is licking my face. Boom has her jaws gently around my wrists, tugging me up. Mouse is several places at the same time. Once she yanks my arm. Then she slaps me. But my body is like a metal blanket too heavy to lift. I can see Mouse's hand, hear the noise of the slap, but I feel nothing. Boom shoves me with her cold wet nose. This I feel.

We are down to minutes, and we don't have the black box.

India hoists me, carrying my front half. Mouse tries to drag my legs with her one good arm. It isn't storming out anymore. The sky is overcast, a dull gloomy gray, but it's calm like we are in our own tinted glass room. The weather can't reach us. Nothing can reach us. We follow Boom through the field with my sisters half carrying me.

Boom barks. She's agitated. She runs around in circles half whining, half howling.

"India!" Mouse shouts. "How much time do we have?"

We follow the dog. The blue-eyed dog with one trailing bandage. There's a *beep, beep, beep*, I hear it now.

She leads us to a landslide of rubble. Metal springs, dust, dirt, smoking pieces of a motor still running, an overhead compartment, a suitcase burst at the seams, a man sleeping with his eyes open. His clock is still in his hand. It says 0:00.

"That's the man with the green socks," Mouse says.

I look down at his ankles—Mouse is right, they are green—and up again at his eyes. I remember my father that day. But now I'm older. I know what this means. I hope Mouse does not.

Boom stands barking next to a big piece of twisted aluminum. Under it I see the corner of an orange box.

My eyesight is hazy, dipping in and out. I fight to stay clear. Mouse shakes me and for a minute that helps.

I try to understand, but there's a roaring river in my head that is washing the words away. I need to let go, let the river take me down. India slaps me. Hard, stinging slaps. "Finn, you have eleven minutes left. DO YOU HEAR ME?" she shouts.

I am moving. They are trying to carry me. My sisters love me. They love me very much.

I try to focus on Mouse's curly red hair. Her freckles look funny, like they are jumping out at me. The orange box is sitting on the ground exactly as the wrist screen showed it would be.

"It's here!" Mouse shouts.

How do we get it open? It's as solid and tightly closed as a brick.

"Maybe we could bang it against the ground," India cries.

But Boom is barking again—barking at another box. This box is cracked in two, revealing a small black box inside.

I force my eyes open. I see the box, but just beyond I see the white courtesy phone, sitting on a heap of rubble.

I have seven minutes left. I could pick up the phone. I could go to work for Sparky. He has all the facts I will ever need. His world makes sense. There are no surprises. I wouldn't have to worry again.

But there would be nothing worth worrying about.

No Mom, no India, no Mouse, no Uncle Red. Nothing that mattered at all.

Inside the orange box, the small black box has buttons. I push the one that says *play*. Nothing happens. India pushes *rewind* and a squeaking noise like weird Martian syllables breaks the silence. They pick up speed, then click to a stop. She pushes *play* again.

It sounds like cockpit noise, like an airplane flying, like a man's voice. Slowly the sounds sort themselves into words.

"Push up! Way up! Climb! Climb! Climb! Now, now, now!"

My head is clear. I focus with everything I have inside me. Force my mind to get a grip on my body.

"We have to climb!" I shout.

India turns around, her eyes full of shock. Her voice is shaking like she's hyperventilating. "A tree?"

"A tree big enough for all of us." My voice is coming through loudly now.

There are trees everywhere, but the branches are so high India can't reach them.

Three minutes left. She hasn't found one yet. She's running around crazy, checking the same trees she's already checked.

Two minutes now.

"That one!" I shout. I'm pointing to a tree with one low branch and a huge spread of branches and leaves up top—a canopy with room for all of us. I make it there,

234

but Mouse's arm is broken. She can't climb. She makes little pained squeaks as she tries to pull herself up with her good arm. I breathe down deep into strength I didn't know I had and together India and I heave her up. "Up farther," India shouts, shoving Mouse's blue corduroy pockets. Mouse pulls and we get her all the way up.

I climb after her, just as I start to lose control of my arms. They begin to wobble as if they're turning to liquid, but with the whole force of what matters to me, I get them back.

India is next to me now. Mouse folds my hand around the branch and then India's hand binds us all three to the tree.

"Hold on." I force the words out of my throat, when a deafening boom blows my ear canals out of my head. "Hold on!" I yell as heat rolls in suddenly, unbearably.

The trees sway wildly from the great torch of heat. My skin can't drip sweat fast enough. Mouse huddles against the trunk. India is barely gripping the branch, her legs hanging down. With a great heave, she swings them up.

And then a fireball is unleashed, racing toward us— the size of a house and headed straight for our tree.

"Farther . . . go up farther!" I scream, but the fire is a blinding ball, a yellow-orange explosion of flame ballooning toward us. I grab Mouse, my arm shaking wildly.

The branches will catch fire. The tree will go up in

flames. The embers crackle and fly, trying like evil fingers to touch our tree. The tree to the left bursts into a blue, then yellow, explosion of flame. The fire hisses. The tree to the right explodes like a firecracker, a star exploding in the smoky light.

Mouse's shoe slips off. It drops into the smoky abyss. We do not hear it land.

CHAPTER 35
BLUE SHOE

I t was the dog that found those kids. The shepherd I'd been trying to get rid of. Scrawny and too smart for her own good. Not much of a farm dog either. She showed up one day, paws all dinged up. I didn't much want her, got my three already—so I bandaged her real good and found a town family to take her in, but by nightfall she was back. Every time I'd get her all set with a new home she'd run to our place, hurt paws and all. Nice homes too—the kind that gives their dogs collars with fancy jewels and every kind of doggy treat. But no, she'd be back in a day, maybe two.

After a while, I quit trying. No getting rid of her, once she got it in her mind she was ours. Started calling

237

her Boom, short for Boomerang because of the way she always come back.

Anyways, the plane went down—some kind of bird strike, they think, though they won't know for sure until they find the black box. The plane lost radio contact, seemed to vanish off the radar screen. A big 727 like that don't just *poof* disappear. Everyone and their brother was looking for it. We're the closest spot to the big reserve where they thought the flight went down, so we saw it all. Those with people on the plane, they were out of their minds with worrying. They were all over town with news folks coming in a swarm behind them.

Two of them came to our place, knocked on the door. A big guy with red hair. That was his name too, Red. And the mother of three of them kids I saw on TV. I couldn't understand why she had all three of her kids on the flight when she wasn't on it. City people is different, I guess.

The mom, she kept talking about geography. India, Switzerland, Finland. I couldn't follow until I finally figured out it was her kids' names. But then she said she just knows in her gut they's alive. Moms know that kind of thing. I'm the same with my two.

Maybe city folks ain't so different. They love their kids even if they do have a strange way of showing it, naming them after foreign countries and sending them on plane flights all by themselves. Still, I felt for her.

It was something else she said that stuck in my mind

real good. Her youngest one was interested in planets and she was smart. Said she had blue corduroys and blue sneakers that probably had a few coins in them. I guess she liked to carry dimes in her shoes.

Oh, there was a lot of other stuff too. Her son played basketball, her daughter was in the church choir and counting the days until she got her driver's license. They was moving to the uncle's up in Fort Baker, times being tough now and all. She was asking if I'd get my Ben to look with his crop duster.

Of course I said I would. "Benjamin Bean," I told my Ben, "the corn can wait. You got to look for these kids." Just about everybody in town did their bit.

But the blue shoes with the dimes—that stuck with me.

When I was fixing to feed the dogs, I was cleaning their bowls when Boom, that skinny German shepherd, sets a dusty blue, kid-size sneaker on my foot.

Boom is an odd dog. Don't come up for a love the way the other ones do. Acts more like a cat. Comes in with dead mice, squirrels, rats, lays 'em at my feet like I'm supposed to be happy about it. But when I pick up this shoe, to take it out to the rubbish heap, something jingles. And sure enough, there were dimes taped to the inside just like that mom said and I remembered about the little girl.

Ben Bean, he was in our plane looking for the kids. So I gave Boom the shoe and I hopped in the truck and I'll be darned if that dog didn't lead me straight to those

239

kids. Hundreds of people hunting for them, but the only one knew where they were was a skinny old dog ought to be livin' in town.

Guess where she found 'em. Sittin' in a tree. Yep. All three buckled in like the flight was still going on. They was alive too. Not conscious, but alive. The older girl had her hand so tight around the branch we couldn't hardly pry it off. She was holding all three of their hands together, it looked to me. The little girl with just the one blue shoe had her arm in a homemade sling made from the boy's sweatshirt. Can't imagine how they did that. But they was right, because that arm was broke in three places.

The boy was the one worried me the most. He had his head at a funny angle didn't seem natural, plus he was missing his sweatshirt on account of it was the little girl's sling. Colder than the devil out there. March can surprise you that way. Think winter's over but it ain't. All of 'em frostbit something fierce, but they was alive.

About the only ones who survived the crash were kids. The TV said kids is the ones that make it if anyone do. I'm not sure what happened with them other two they found, but the Tompkins kids' seats were all three bound together. They was thrown clear and the canopy of branches caught them like a big old tree hand. Probably wouldn't have if they'd been the size of my two, but they wasn't so big yet and they was just hanging there when Boom found them.

With that fuel on board the rest of the plane exploded.

Some kind of fireball, I reckon. It was a miracle those kids didn't burn up. A miracle their mom told me about the dimes. A miracle Boom let me know where they was at. That's three miracles. Most folks don't ever get but one.

Course it coulda been something else too. Somethin' on the inside makes one person want to save himself where the next one just gives on up. Can't give someone that or take it away neither. Just the way they's put together.

I saw them after they was better too. Went to the hospital over in Denver the day they got out. They was nice kids, real polite. And that Uncle Red, he's good folks—loves 'em almost as much as their mom, you can see that plain as day.

While I was in Denver I did my own little crazy. Being around those city folks done it, I guess, because on my way home I spent my cookie jar money on one of them fancy collars with glued-on jewels for my Boom. The way I figure it, a dog saves three kids, she deserves something real special. You bet she do.

ACKNOWLEDGMENTS

No Passengers Beyond This Point seemed to come out of nowhere, yet looking back I see how many people contributed to its creation.

It started with Lori Benton, who was determined to have a book with a smart, six-year-old protagonist. I had no intention of writing the book she wanted—none at all—and then Mouse appeared. How did Lori know she was in there?

Once Mouse, Finn, and India found their story, the manuscript went to Kathy Dawson, who worked relentlessly draft after draft to help me bring reason to an unreasonable narrative. Kathy possesses her own special ESP for manuscripts—able to discern and develop what isn't yet there. She could have governed a small country in the time it took to edit this book. I will always be indebted to her for her thoughtful comments. Working with her is just plain fun.

Getting the novel in shape would not have been possible without the help of our expert readers. First to hear bits and pieces were the astute ladies in my crit group: Alla Crone, Ella Thorp Ellis, Patsy Garlan, and Zilpha Keatley Snyder. And then came my heavy-hitter readers: my best writer friend—Barbara Kerley, one of the smartest librarians I know—Angela Reynolds, and the powerhouse readers at Penguin: Claire Evans, Jessica Garrison, Jen Haller, Emily Heddleson, Lauri Hornik, and Alisha Niehaus. Thanks for the honest and thoughtful input of each of you.

Along the way we had help from the gracious Elizabeth Harding and the team at Curtis-Brown, plus we got guidance about the title from school groups in Portland and Petaluma in Cleveland, Clayton and Corte Madera.

Through it all my husband, Jacob, cheered me on, my son, Ian, let me borrow his favorite sponge story, and my daughter, Kai, begged to read each draft. Thank you, thank you, thank you, what a gift you all are to me.

By the same author

Shortlisted for the Carnegie Medal

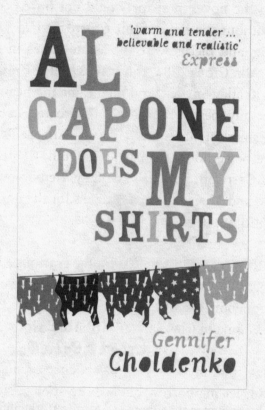

'Warm and tender, believable and realistic' *Express*

'Gennifer Choldenko is a bright light in teenage fiction'
Independent

By the same author

'This sequel is ingenious . . . terrific storytelling'
The Times

'Cleverly constructed and compulsively readable'
Books for Keeps